THE COWBOY
SEAL'S TRIPLETS

BY
TINA LEONARD

MILLS &
BOON

Published in Great Britain 2015
by Mills & Boon, an imprint of Harlequin (UK) Limited,
Eton House, 18-24 Paradise Road, Richmond, Surrey, TW9 1SR

© 2015 Tina Leonard

ISBN: 978-0-263-25153-1

23-0715

Harlequin (UK) Limited's policy is to use papers that are natural, renewable and recyclable products and made from wood grown in sustainable forests. The logging and manufacturing processes conform to the legal environmental regulations of the country of origin.

Printed and bound in Spain
by CPI, Barcelona

Tina Leonard is a *USA TODAY* bestselling and award-winning author of more than fifty projects, including several popular miniseries for the Mills & Boon® Cherish™ line. Known for bad-boy heroes and smart, adventurous heroines, her books have made the *USA TODAY*, Waldenbooks, Ingram and Nielsen BookScan bestseller lists. Born on a military base, Tina lived in many states before eventually marrying the boy who did her crayon printing for her in the first grade. You can visit her at www.tinaleonard.com, and follow her on Facebook and Twitter.

For the many wonderful readers who so enthusiastically
and kindly supported my work from day one—
I thank you from the bottom of my heart.

Chapter One

John Lopez "Squint" Mathison came roaring into town with Daisy Donovan on the back of his motorcycle, making all the good citizens of Bridesmaids Creek, Texas, buzz like bees in a beehive. The five men who were in love with Daisy—her gang, consisting of Carson Dare, Gabriel Conyers, Clint Shanahan, Red Holmes and Dig Bailey—followed behind them in a truck, with Daisy's infamous motorcycle secured in the truck bed.

It was a very strange sight not to see Daisy riding her own bike. No one could remember ever seeing her on the back of someone else's, and the gossip flew fast and thick.

Squint was ready to see the last of Daisy's gang. And maybe even Daisy herself, despite the fact that she'd once possessed his heart and his romantic dreams.

What he'd been thinking, he wasn't certain.

She was completely wild, as everyone in Bridesmaids Creek had always tried to warn him.

The trouble was, he'd made love to Daisy Donovan while they were in Montana, in a weak moment when he shouldn't have let his stupid heart outstrip his good sense.

Making love to Daisy had been even more mind-bending than he could have ever imagined. Then the five Romeos had blown into Montana to retrieve their small-town wild child princess, and Squint had seen that they were—himself included—all dopes dangling after a prize they couldn't win.

At that moment, he'd decided to come back to Bridesmaids Creek, check in on his buddies and shift off to the rodeo. After the rodeo, if his heart was still bleeding, he thought maybe he'd get a job teaching ROTC or something, somewhere far away. He'd make those decisions as soon as Valentine's Day was past, although he couldn't have said why Cupid's Big Day was his marker for a quiet exit.

Daisy hopped off the bike as soon as he came to a stop in front of the main house at the Hanging H Ranch. "Thanks for the ride."

"No problem."

"It was great seeing the country from a motorcycle. No windows to block the view." She shook her long, dark locks out of her helmet. "But it's wonderful to be home."

He nodded and headed into the kitchen to find his friends—the men that he could always count on to talk sense into him. Daisy followed, which was a surprise. Wherever Daisy went, so did her love-struck gang, so they came, too.

"I'm so glad to be back in BC," Daisy said, and Squint started. "Montana is beautiful, but after a while, I began craving the comforts of small-town life."

This was news to him. Squint wished he hadn't fallen head, heels and heart for Daisy, and had put plenty of distance between him and her gang perching at the kitchen island. The gang gathered around the kitchen island, which had over the years become the communal gathering place and feed bag summit. No one ever knocked on the back door of the Hanging H; they just let themselves in.

If you weren't family or friend, you rang the front doorbell—not a good sign in a small town where everyone knew everybody else, and their business. Ringing the front bell meant you were an outsider.

Robert Donovan, Daisy's father, always rang the doorbell. Somehow his daughter had managed it so that she considered herself part of the backdoor squad. Very recently, indeed—and Squint wasn't sure why his poor mushy heart suddenly wished he had his own back door that she could make herself at home through anytime she liked.

But he'd never been one for settling down, never had a "real" home that wasn't on wheels, so he shoved that thought out of his brain, a useless organ that did little to assist him with rational thinking where Daisy was concerned. Out of habit, he shifted the Saint Michael medal he wore, trying to figure out his next move.

"I wonder where Mackenzie and Suz are?" Squint peered into the living room for the house's owners and their husbands, Justin Morant and Cisco Grant—Frog to his friends, though his wife, Suz, had let everyone know that she wasn't kissing a Frog, hence the Cisco. Squint was a nickname, too, given to him for his shooting skills, which were far better than Cupid's as far as he was concerned. Maybe it was time for him, too, to change his moniker back to his real name. Was it more likely that Daisy would fall for "John" rather than "Squint"?

Suz had not been easy for Cisco to catch, but catch

her he had, and they'd celebrated that love for a second time last Christmas Eve. This was February—and who would have thought that only two months after Cisco's wedding, John would have made love to Daisy Donovan, the woman who drove everybody absolutely nuts in Bridesmaids Creek. And he hadn't just done it once—she'd sneaked into his bed many times, all under cover of night.

He had been completely aware she wasn't about to let a sign of their new relationship hit the public domain, especially not since she'd mooned after Cisco for months and months. John was aware that Daisy felt as if she was settling by making love to him, and not as in settling down—just settling. Making do.

He was done with that. He'd tried to "win" her fair and square, by Bridesmaids Creek standards, which meant either running the Best Man's Fork, or swimming the Bridesmaids Creek swim in order to win the love of your life. This was a no-fail charm, according to BC legend. But Daisy'd had three chances at the magic, and no time had he ever won her. Apparently the magic didn't work so well for him. A man had to push forward, even if his dreams were in ruins. He'd learned the hard way when he'd served in Afghanistan with Sam and Cisco that with life you have to keep going.

And he would keep going now. In fact, to make certain there were no more loose moments, he was making sure Daisy was parked here for good—then he was leaving town for the rodeo circuit. It was the only way. The second option would be to just cut out his heart and throw it to the wolves somewhere—that would end the pain of knowing that Daisy was only making time with him, even though she'd admitted that she'd never loved Cisco in the slightest. She'd only been after him to keep him from Suz.

Which hadn't worked. Suz and Cisco now had darling twin girls, and the magic of Bridesmaids Creek had cast its happy spell on them.

"Ah, cookies," Dig Bailey said. "It's great to be home."

John took that in without comment. The Hanging H had never been Dig's home, and never would be.

I should have taken Daisy to her house, and left her and her gang behind. Then I could start to forget the colossal mistake I made when I fell into her sexy brown eyes the day I met her.

"I missed the cocoa," Carson Dare said, helping himself to some that was staying warm in a heated pitcher.

John could barely think about cocoa. He tried hard not to watch Daisy settle her delicately shaped, feminine assets on a stool at the island. It was terribly difficult to keep his eyes off her.

The first time he'd ever seen Daisy Donovan—at times known as the Diva of Destruction of Bridesmaids Creek—he'd been captivated by her long dark hair spilling from her motorcycle helmet, her heart-shaped lips, big expresso eyes that practically bewitched his soul, never mind the short black leather skirt that swung when she walked. She'd been wearing black combat boots and her shapely legs had transfixed him, making his brain a pile of ham salad.

Life hadn't changed a whole lot since then.

"Chocolate chip cake," Clint Shanahan said, sighing happily as he helped himself to a piece.

Red Holmes joined him and cut a slice for himself. "There's no place like home, just like Dorothy said."

"Listen, you fellows should probably follow the yellow brick road right on out of here," John said sourly. "I didn't see a kitchen's open sign on the back door."

They all stared at him.

"We're from this town," Gabriel Conyers said. "We know when we're welcome. Do you?"

Point well taken. John was the outsider, though employed at the Hanging H for the past three years.

"Besides which, you just want to get Daisy alone," Carson said, "and we've determined amongst ourselves that we're going to make sure that doesn't happen."

"True," Dig agreed. "She may not choose us, but we're not letting you weasel her, either."

Too late, fellows, the weasel's already been to the henhouse. Several times.

"I'm going to the bunkhouse." Since Justin and Cisco weren't here, it was highly likely they were there. Although John was a bit surprised that Suz and Mackenzie weren't around with their plethora of babies. Between them, they had six now at the Hanging H—all girls destined to break young men's hearts.

Something he knew too well about. John shoved his hat on his head, glared at Daisy's gang, and without bothering to look at Daisy, went out the back door. Unable to stop himself, he went around to the front, his boots crunching through the snow piled around the front porch. He wanted just a moment to take in the house, maybe even take a photo on his phone—because he was about to leave forever. There was no point in waiting until V-Day, because Cupid's Arrow Delivery Service wasn't going to bring him an arrow with Daisy's name on it. This was the only real home he'd ever known. Permanent home, to be more precise. When you'd grown up in a beat-up trailer following the rodeo from town to town, home didn't feel as if it had a stationary place. His parents had raised three children that way, and they'd grown up fine.

He supposed he and Daisy, the daughter of the richest man in Bridesmaids Creek, didn't have a whole lot of common ground, anyway—which was why she'd never particularly gone for him, except under cover of darkness. John's father and his grandfather and his father before him had been clowns and barrel men, with the occasional bullfighter gig thrown into the mix. His mother was a cowboy preacher, her three boys sitting in the front pews without fail.

Maybe that was why the Hanging H meant so much to him. It was permanent. Well, it had almost *not* been permanent, thanks to Daisy and her greedy father, Robert. John raised his phone, snapping a photo of the snow-laden house. It was tall and white in Victorian splendor, its heavy gingerbread detail charming and old-world. Four tall turrets stretched to the sky, and the upstairs mullioned windows sparkled in the sunshine. The wide wraparound porch was painted sky blue, and a white wicker sofa with blue cushions beckoned visitors to sit and enjoy the view. A collection of wrought-iron roosters sat nearby in a welcoming clutch, and the bristly doormat with a big burgundy *H* announced the Hawthorne name, which Suz and Mackenzie had been before their marriages. Their parents had built this farm up years ago, as well as the business they'd started here—the Haunted H, a popular carnival and play place for families.

Nothing had changed, which was comforting. And Robert Donovan hadn't managed to take over the Hanging H, though he and Daisy had given it plenty of effort.

Sometimes John felt as if he'd been in lust with the enemy. He was just so drawn to Daisy, it was as if all that bad-girl-calling vibe shook him down to his knees.

There'd been something of a happy ending, as recently as December, when Suz and Cisco had retied the knot. Robert Donovan had had some kind of epiphany, deciding that he didn't want to be the town bully anymore, and sold the Hanging H back to Suz and Mackenzie for a dollar—though he'd moved heaven and hell to take over the property in the beginning.

Rumor had it that Daisy had turned, deciding she was no longer going to be the Diva of Destruction, and convinced her father—who was already developing a huge soft spot due to his newly acquired desire to be considered a beloved grandfather—that he didn't want to be the town Grinch anymore.

John snapped one last photo, sighed at the memories of the only place that had ever felt like a true home to him, and put his phone away. Then he headed off without another look back, to return to the only other home he'd ever known.

A small trailer he'd recently heard was somewhere just outside of Santa Fe.

He'd be safe there—safe from his heart begging him to make love to Daisy anytime night fell to cover their sin.

"WHAT DO YOU MEAN, he just left?" Daisy hopped off her stool and ran to the window. Sure enough, there went Squint's truck, hauling down the drive fast enough to make the truck bed lurch. A little concern jumped inside her, but then she calmed it. No doubt he'd just gone to grab a bite at The Wedding Diner. Or gone to see Madame and Monsieur Matchmaker—though now that they were divorced, perhaps it was fair to say that they were no longer Bridesmaids Creek's special matchmakers. Daisy gulped. That split could probably be laid square at her and her father's door, as they'd taken over the establishment where Madame Matchmaker's Premier Matchmaking Services, and Monsieur Unmatchmaker's Services, had once been housed. Now her gang had the space, and they'd put in a hopping cigar bar, sort of a pickup meet-and-get-sweet kind of place that doubled as a dating service and hangout.

There was no going back now.

Somehow she'd have to win the townspeople over, make up for a lot of the wrong she'd done. Daisy went back to sit with her gang, looking around at the five men who professed themselves in love with her.

"Listen, fellows. We've had a long, good run together." Daisy took a deep breath. "But things are going to have to change."

"Change?" Gabriel sat up. "What kind of change?"

There'd have to be lots of change if she was going to convince Bridesmaids Creek that she was a new woman. "Change. As much as possible."

"I don't like it." Red shook his head. "We've got a great thing going, the six of us."

Yes, but they didn't know that she'd been diving under the sheets with Squint. And the lovemaking was fantastic. Mind-blowing. Once she'd gotten through the smoke and haze of trying to keep Suz and Cisco apart—what had she been thinking?—she'd realized the hunky, tall, saddle-brown-eyed Squint was a really sexy guy. Supersexy, to the point of being mouthwatering. And when he kissed her, she melted. Like a puddle of snow in hot sun. "It can't be the six of us anymore."

They looked alarmed. "But we're so good together," Carson said.

She shook her head. "Actually, we're not. We were the misfits and outcasts together. But that's not what I want to be anymore."

"Whoa," Clint said. "It's Squint, isn't it? John Lopez Mathison is getting inside your head."

Daisy jumped. "Of course not!"

"It was Branch Winters," Dig said darkly. "Every time you go to Montana to his retreat, you change. That was when it started, when you went chasing up there after Cisco. You came home different."

"Yeah," Red said. "You came home not mooning after Cisco anymore. And not really wanting to hang out with us, either."

Daisy got up. They were right, of course. Branch's place in Montana was a spiritual retreat where warriors of all kinds went to reboot. She'd gone to throw a few wrenches into Cisco's works—and found a few thrown in hers instead. It was hard to explain Branch. He sort of lived on the metaphysical, and sometimes hippie, edge of life—but he'd helped her see that she was operating out of fear of never belonging in Bridesmaids Creek.

And only she could change that.

"It's going to be okay, for all of us," Daisy said softly, going to the door. "But change is in the wind. It has to be."

She went outside into the cold February chill, knowing this was the right path—if she was ever going to make John Lopez "Squint" Mathison believe that it was *him* with whom she'd been in love all along.

She didn't know if there was enough magic in Bridesmaids Creek to convince him, but she had to try.

Chapter Two

Daisy felt every eye on her as she walked into The Wedding Diner the next morning. She was aware the town didn't have a very high opinion of her, even though she'd managed to convince her father to give up pursuing the Hanging H, and even though she'd talked him into giving up on taking over the land where the Best Man's Fork and Bridesmaids Creek lay in sleepy, small-town fashion. The Hawthorne's Haunted H amusement park for kiddies was now situated on some land near Bridesmaids Creek, because Daisy had convinced the Hawthorne sisters that no one could take over their home and their business all at once if they weren't tied together. Now the year-round haunted house was more of a community venture, which helped everyone in BC, because it was more centrally located, and people were assigned regular hours to run it. It was more lucrative for the town now, and with time, Daisy thought that its popularity would only grow.

But memories were long in BC, and she'd done an awful lot of bad. She smiled at everyone who turned to stare at her, and moved into a white vinyl booth that Jane Chatham, who owned The Wedding Diner, showed her to.

"You're back," Jane said, and Daisy nodded.

"We came back yesterday, Squint, myself and the boys."

Jane's gaze was steady on her. "Squint left town last night."

Daisy blinked. "Left town?"

The older woman hesitated, then sat across from her. Cosette Lafleur—Madame Matchmaker herself—slid in next to Jane, her pink-frosted hair accentuating her all-knowing eyes.

Daisy's heart sank. "He *couldn't* have left." He hadn't said goodbye, hadn't even mentioned he was planning to make like a stiff breeze and blow away.

The women stared at her with interest.

"Did you want him to stay, Daisy?" Jane asked.

"Well—" Daisy began, not knowing how to say that she'd thought she at least rated a "goodbye" considering she'd gotten quite in the habit of enjoying a nocturnal meeting in his arms. "It would have been nice."

"Have you finally realized where your heart belongs, Daisy?" Cosette asked, and Daisy started.

"My heart?" How was it that these women always seemed to read everyone's mind? A girl had to be very careful to keep her secrets tight to her chest. "Squint and I are friends."

Cosette winked at her, and a spark of hope lit inside Daisy that maybe Cosette wasn't horribly angry or holding a grudge with her about the whole taking-over-her-shop mistake she'd made.

"We know all about those kinds of friends," Cosette said, nodding wisely.

"Still," Jane said, "it does seem rather heartless of John to leave without telling you. Had you quarreled?"

Here it came, the well-meaning BC interference of which many suffered, all secretly cherished and she'd never had the benefit of experiencing. She had to say it was like being under a probing yet somehow friendly microscope. "We didn't quarrel."

"But you're in love with him," Cosette said.

"That may be putting it a bit—" Her words trailed off.

"Mildly?" Jane asked.

"Lightly?" Cosette said. "You are in fact head over heels in love with him?"

Daisy felt herself blush under all the scrutiny. Sheriff Dennis McAdams slid into the booth next to her, and the ladies wasted no time filling in the sheriff, who turned his curious gaze to her.

"He left last night," the sheriff said, and Daisy wondered if John Lopez Mathison had stopped by to see every single denizen of this town to say goodbye— except for her.

"Yes, I've heard," Daisy said.

"Not coming back, either," the sheriff continued. "Jane, can I get some of your delicious double-dipped chicken-fried steak and mashed red potatoes with gravy? Maybe chase it with a slice of your four-layer chocolate cake?"

"Gracious," Cosette said, "are you looking to have a four-alarm cardiac event, Dennis?"

"Just hungry, ladies." He pushed back his worn Stetson with a grin. "Sitting up late at night with the fellows, having a good gossip and four-tissue wheeze gives a man an appetite."

Jane eyed him with great curiosity. "A four-tissue wheeze requires a slice of four-layer chocolate cake?"

"Yes, ma'am." Dennis nodded. "Squint was really working on my ear holes. As were Sam, Phillipe and Robert Donovan."

"I don't believe a word of it," Cosette said. "I can't see you five ever getting together for a rooster session."

"It happened," Dennis said cheerfully. "The first order of business was Squint requesting that we call him John from here on. After all, Squint was his military name, and he's gone back to being a cowboy. So, John it is. But the big news of the evening was Robert Donovan announcing he feels greatly that his daughter, our Daisy here," he said, winking at Daisy, "needs a man."

"What?" Daisy shook her head. "My father would never say such a thing. I'm with Cosette. This gathering never took place."

"He wants a man to settle you here in town, far away from the influence of whatever is happening in Montana," Dennis continued, untroubled by the ladies' disbelief. "And I said there was no such man to do the job in this small town."

"And?" Jane demanded, not leaving to put in the sheriff's order, Daisy noticed. When the gossip was flying hot and steamy, food took a backseat. "What was said to Robert's grand pronouncement?"

Dennis shrugged, very much enjoying being the center of the ladies' attention. "John said he agreed with me, and—"

"What?" Daisy stiffened. "How dare he?"

They all looked at her.

"How dare he, what, dear?" Jane asked.

"How dare John agree with my father?" Daisy thought

the former Squint Mathison might have reached a new level of annoying.

"Most folks rather agree with Robert," Cosette said, nodding.

"So what happened then?" Jane demanded.

"Could you put my order in before I tell you the rest?" Dennis asked, rubbing his stomach regretfully. "I didn't have breakfast."

"Sing for your supper, Sheriff," Jane shot back.

"Well, I was pretty proud of my two cents, I don't mind saying," Dennis said. "And then Sam said that he didn't think even he had the necessary talent to pull off the job."

"What job?" Daisy asked, her heart beginning an emergency tattoo. It sounded as if all the important men in her life—notwithstanding Sam Barr, otherwise known as Handsome Sam, and understood by all to be a trickster and prankster beyond compare—had clubbed together and cast her to the wind. "Pardon me, but I'm having great trouble seeing my father and my…my—"

"Your what, dear?" Jane Chatham asked, her eyes twinkling with interest.

"My…good friend John," Daisy said, covering herself. "I have trouble seeing the two of them agreeing on anything, but certainly my father wouldn't spend any time discussing my love life with my—"

"With your good friend John," Cosette said. "Yes, yes, yes, we heard all that."

"And yet, it happened," Sheriff Dennis said. "Now may I have that supper for which I sang like a many-feathered bird?"

"Not really," Daisy said as Jane and Cosette nodded in agreement that the sheriff hadn't quite imparted sufficiently satisfactory details. Daisy's heart rate was still revving as she began to realize that the men had sold her out and the one she'd been spending delicious nights with had slipped out without saying a word to her. "What was the point of this male bonding?"

The sheriff smiled. "You know how it is when we fellows get together. We just hash out life, come to no solutions and feel like we've accomplished something."

"A solution was achieved if John's gone," Daisy said.

"He is gone," Dennis said. "Said something about returning to his home."

"He doesn't have a home," Jane said, "other than the Hanging H, which is his home now."

"Oh, he has a home," Dennis said, "it's just not one you and I would really think of as one. His is on the rodeo circuit."

"All the men say that," Cosette said, huffing out a breath impatiently. "They always claim rodeo is their hearth, heart and home."

"In John's case, it's true." Dennis looked wistfully toward the kitchen. "His family is now heading toward Santa Fe, apparently, hauling along the family domicile. Rather like a circus train, I suppose."

"What in the world are you talking about?" Cosette demanded.

"John's family follows the rodeo. That's how they make their living." Dennis shrugged. "His mom's a cowboy preacher, and his dad and brothers are bullfighters and barrel men, going back generations. They've got a little motor home that they go from town to town in."

"Rather a gypsy-ish lifestyle, isn't it?" Jane asked, and Daisy's heart sank. Just hearing this description of John's home life made her realize that he might, conceivably, never darken the doors of Bridesmaids Creek again.

"Yep," Dennis said, "and he's not coming back. Not anytime soon, anyway."

There was no way she could let that happen. Not after she'd finally come to her senses, after all the many moons of not realizing what a catch Squint—*John*—really was, hiding under all that brown-eyed, gentle bear exterior. Daisy swallowed hard, realizing the people sitting around the table were studying her, waiting silently for her to speak up.

Maybe it did serve her right to have John desert her for good after the many times he'd tried to win her. But she wasn't the kind of woman who gave up—in fact, there were some who said that adversity only strengthened her will.

"You realize, Daisy, there won't be a race run or a swim swum for you," Jane said gently. "I'm afraid you threw away your three chances."

"She didn't *throw* them away," Cosette said, her eyes softening as she looked at Daisy. Daisy felt this was very sweet of Cosette, especially as much of Cosette's hard luck was Daisy's fault. "She merely misplaced her three chances. Magic is *never* gone forever."

Daisy paused. Of course. She was a Bridesmaids Creek girl, even if she'd come to town late, at the age of three. The magic would still work for her—it *had* to.

Because John made love to her like no man ever could, and it might have taken her way too long to realize it, but she knew in every corner of her heart that she was in love with him.

"I'm going to need help," Daisy said softly. "I could really use some assistance in figuring out the right way to convince John that leaving Bridesmaids Creek wasn't his best decision."

They all took that in.

"We're always here for one of our hometown girls," Dennis said solemnly, and the ladies nodded, and Daisy felt warmed just by being designated a "hometown" girl. Maybe forgiveness was possible after all. She sure hoped so.

Now she just had to convince John that his home was here, and not the place where he'd grown up.

Rodeo.

JOHN FOUND HIS parents and brothers just outside of Santa Fe. Their small silver mobile home rumbled under turquoise-colored skies, with a truck—his brothers'—following closely behind. If not for cell phone contact, he would have missed them.

Mary and Mack Mathison waved at him as he pulled alongside their white truck, which hauled the silver Airstream mobile home they'd bought too many years ago for John to remember. His brothers Javier and Jackson saluted him, and he fell back into position, trailing behind the white truck lettered *Mathison* on both doors in black. Home sweet home.

This was it. He turned on some tunes, tried not to think about Daisy and told himself he was content to caravan as far away from Texas as possible.

"This could never have been her life," John told the smiling bobblehead dog on his dash. "Daisy grew up with so much wealth, so much of everything, that she couldn't possibly understand this kind of pared-down existence."

The black-and-white bobblehead dog he'd named Joe,

because it fit the *J* motif of his and his brothers' names, neither agreed nor disagreed. In fact, Joe didn't seem to be worried about much of anything other than the sunburn he was getting on his furry behind, courtesy of dash sitting. John watched the mountains of New Mexico fade away, thought about how beautiful it would be to see this highway on his motorcycle, with Daisy parked comfortably on the back, her arms around his waist, which she'd done all the way back from Montana. He got a woody just remembering her delicate arms around him, felt a dull hammer begin inside his skull.

"Holy Christmas," John muttered. "I'm going to have to take up serious meditation to get her out of my head."

He'd left his motorcycle in Bridesmaids Creek, under Sam's care, with dire instructions that it was to be in the same beloved condition when he returned. Sam had agreed with a grin, saying smartly that of course it looked even better with Daisy polishing the seat, and would he mind—

"At which point I gave Sam such a glare that he shut clean up," John told Joe, and Joe nodded in approval. Or maybe he didn't nod in approval, but if he wasn't nodding in approval, then what the hell good was a bobble-head dog to a man, anyway?

At the border connecting New Mexico and Colorado, his parents stopped the caravan at a roadside rest stop. He hadn't expected them to stop so soon, as life on the road was about putting the miles between destinations. But they were more than happy to halt the train soon after he'd joined them, to welcome him back to the fold.

"What the hell, son?" Mack demanded, giving him a tight hug. "You took a year off my life showing up like that. I thought I'd seen a ghost."

"Might as well be a ghost," Mary said. "He hasn't been around in four years."

His brothers banged him on the back with enthusiasm. "We missed the hell out of you," Javier said.

"We've been keeping Mack and Mary on the circuit," Jackson said. "It'll be good to have you back. You can help us keep them focused. They keep wanting to run off to New Zealand."

"New Zealand?" John looked at his parents as they began checking over the ancient trailer. There was never much time for idle conversation. Everyone had their chores and responsibilities at each stop, where duties were parceled out and executed with a minimum of discussion. It was all business: check the equipment, use the facilities, stretch the legs and get back in the trucks.

As a child, John had carried along a soccer ball to kick with his brothers at the stops. He'd always wished they could stop long enough to have a real picnic at one of the shaded tables that usually graced a rest stop. On their birthdays, they did—but as a rule, the road was a demanding mistress, and must be gotten back to immediately.

"It's my birthday," he said suddenly, wanting his parents and brothers to cease their ant-like scurrying, and act as if him showing up in their midst after four years away was actually a big deal.

"Your birthday?" Mary frowned, thinking. "Is it?"

John nodded. "Yes."

"Good heavens," Mack said. "I think he's telling the truth."

"I'm a Navy SEAL," John said. "I lean toward honesty."

They stared at him, perplexed. "It's just that we stay

in our groove," Mary said. "We don't mean to seem uncaring."

"I know." John shrugged. "No big deal. Let's sit down and have a water bottle or something. Talk."

His parents took that in.

"All right, son," Mack said after a long moment. "Javier, do we have any birthday cake in the trailer freezer?"

John sighed, remembering this well. Birthday cakes, of course, were kept in the freezer, for birthdays occurring on the road. No muss, no fuss. And nothing home baked. The boys had been homeschooled, too, which meant a rolling education. But Mary was smart, and they'd learned everything they needed to know to do very well on the standardized tests. At one point, young Javier had even decided he might want to attend college and had applied to Florida State, finding himself a very desirable candidate before he'd ultimately decided he preferred to stay with the family.

That was what happened: you spent your life on the road, and nothing else seemed as exciting.

They sat under one of the awnings at a concrete table. A couple of birds hopped near, wondering if the humans might drop any crumbs. *Pity the bird that thinks it is getting crumbs from the Mathisons*, John thought—feeling bad when Javier came out from the trailer triumphantly bearing five slices of cake, one of them anointed with a lit candle. Javier put this one in front of John, grinning. He whistled a long note, and his family all burst into the "Happy Birthday" song.

"Make a wish!" they exclaimed, so John blew out his candle—totally annoyed with himself when he realized that the image that flickered across his mind the instant he tried to think of what he'd wish for was Daisy's beautiful face.

Before he'd had a chance to stop his brain, he'd wished she were here with him right now.

What a stupid wish.

Chapter Three

John couldn't have been more stunned when Sam's truck pulled up beside the family trailer, but his brain seemed to separate into two parts when Daisy's long-legged sexiness got out of the passenger side.

He shoved his cake with the birthday candle still smoking far away from him—clearly Bridesmaids Creek didn't have the only claim to mystical mayhem—and got up to greet his friend. And the woman who drove him mad even in his sleep.

"What the hell, buddy?" John said to Sam, slapping the bearlike man on the back by way of embrace. Over Sam's shoulder, John's gaze was locked onto Daisy. She smiled, looking a trifle unsure of herself, which was unusual for Daisy. "What brings you two here?"

"Following you," Sam said, then went to say hello to Mr. and Mrs. Mathison, and Javier and Jackson.

That left John staring at Daisy, drowning in her dark eyes. "Hi."

She smiled. "Hello."

"So, is somebody going to tell me what's going on?" John asked.

"You left without saying goodbye."

"How did you find me?"

"It wasn't hard. You told the fellows exactly where you were headed. Sam said we'd just get in the truck and follow the smoke of your truck as you burned rubber out of BC." She frowned. "How could you leave without saying goodbye? After…after we rode on your motorcycle all the way home from Montana?"

That was a nice way of saying *How could you just leave like that after we'd made love like crazy?* John sighed. "I'm sorry. I was probably a heel. Didn't think it through."

"I'd say you didn't." Daisy's frown deepened, and he could tell she was really hurt.

"Daisy, look," he began, "we just don't suit. You know that."

She stared at him silently.

"I mean, we suit *sexually*," he said, lowering his voice, then pulled her farther from the group. His parents would be concerned about getting off schedule, but for the moment, they seemed happy to visit with Sam. Sam, of course, had helped himself to John's slice of cake, casually flinging the candle in the trash. "What happened in Montana is best left in Montana."

Daisy shook her head. "I don't believe that's really what you want."

"Do you see my family, Daze?" He pointed to the trailer. "This is my life, and it's as far away from Bridesmaids Creek and all that crazy magic as it could be. This is real life, this is the real John Lopez 'Squint' Mathison. I ain't no Prince Charming, sweetheart."

"I understand that you're—that you've misunderstood what I need from a man after I chased Cisco, stupidly, of course," Daisy began, but he shook his head.

"I don't even think about that. I knew what was going

on all along. I understood that you were just trying to fit in, and to find your own place in BC. But, Daisy, beautiful as you are, as desirable as you are, I'm not the man for you. I'm sorry." He took a deep breath. "I'm really sorry that you came all this way having to listen to Sam's hot air, too."

"John," Daisy began.

"I'm not going to turn into a handsome, secret prince like Cisco did."

"Cisco's from some kind of minor, minor royal lineage. And that's not why I'm here!"

"But at the time, the idea of a title was dazzling to you, and this," he said, gesturing to the beat-up trailer, "isn't dazzling. It didn't dazzle you then, and it's not going to dazzle you now, but this is my family. This is our way of life." He touched one of her long dark locks ruefully. "And I don't think you're exactly cut out for the migrant sort of life, princess."

She moved his hand. "Thank you for your opinion, but I'm capable of figuring out what I want."

"Because you knew what you wanted last year?" he asked, hating to be an ass but needing to make her see.

She stepped closer. "John, I *know* you care about me."

"Always have, and part of me always will." He moved away from her. "Trust me, Daisy, this would be an even bigger mistake than you and Cisco would have been."

"I was never in love with Cisco. I never cared about him, not the way you think I did." Daisy looked like tears might sprout any second, which was also a very unusual thing for the town's ex-bad girl. "You and I belong together, John Mathison."

He had to give her credit, being a daddy's girl had taught her to go after what she wanted. Or thought she wanted. But John understood human nature, and in this case, Daisy had just turned her gotta-have-it shopping list from one man to another. "Next year, it'll be someone else, beautiful, I promise."

She reached out, lightly touching the Saint Michael medal under his denim shirt. "You and I both know about this medal. You got it from a peddler you met when you and your family were following the rodeo. He told you it would always protect you. All of you SEALs have one, but you and Cisco got yours switched overseas one day at training, and Suz thinks that tangled up something. She said it misplaced the Bridesmaids Creek magic, so that I thought Cisco was the man for me." Daisy took a deep breath. "I'm not sure it happened that way. You've always been the only man for me. In fact, I *know* it in my heart. It just took me too long to see it. But I'm not going to beg you, John." She smacked his chest, right over his heart, and his breath flew from him, his brain shot into outer space and that red corpuscle-driving organ that was trying to deny how much it cared for Daisy seemed to stop beating for just the space of a second. Peace and tranquillity descended upon John just as Daisy walked away from him to go introduce herself to his family—only to be replaced by red-hot lust and fiery passion engulfing his entire soul as he watched her walk away from him. It felt as if he were drowning in desire, as if his impulses were threatening to overtake his good sense. Aching to take back every word he'd said, he rubbed his chest where she'd lightly smacked his heart, willing himself to come back inside his body and be rational, damn it—but he had never really been rational where Daisy

Donovan was concerned, and today was probably not going to be the day he started.

Bridesmaids Creek's reach appeared to be long-ranging.

"I'M FINE," DAISY said as she and Sam got back into his truck. "Thanks for driving me out here to find John's knuckleheaded self."

Sam laughed as he pulled onto the highway. "I told you he'd have his *cabeza* pretty well stuffed up his butt."

"It's a lot of my own fault." Daisy sighed, resisting the urge to glance over her shoulder in the vain hope that John might have had second thoughts about sending her away and was even now charging after Sam's truck. "I chased something I didn't even want too long, and ignored the man who is right for me. I don't blame him for not being entirely convinced that my heart belongs to him."

"So now what?"

"Now," Daisy said on a long breath, "hopefully, I enjoy a healthy pregnancy—"

"What?" Sam slammed on the brakes.

"Don't you *dare* even *think* about turning around and going back."

"But you didn't tell him that! I know you didn't! John would never have let you go if he knew you were pregnant! Are you really expecting a baby?"

"Keep driving," Daisy said in a toneless command. "Yes, I'm expecting a baby."

"Holy crap!" Sam turned the air conditioner on full blast, though the day was chilly and overcast. "Listen, you're going to get me in a whole lot of caca with one John Lopez Mathison. If he finds out that I knew—"

"It's all right, Sam. John's made his choice. I'm not using a baby to change his mind. Absolutely not. And if you tell him," Daisy said, staring at him, "I'll set the matchmakers in town on you."

The gentle bear of a man literally developed a peaked cast under his skin. "You wouldn't!"

"I *would.*"

"I don't want a woman! I don't want a bride. Everyone has long known that I came along with John and Cisco just for the ride. Just to cause trouble, really."

"I'm aware." Daisy nodded. "But troublemakers sometimes find trouble."

He pulled off a ramp and parked in a deserted parking lot that appeared to once have housed shops, but was now long abandoned. "Daisy, listen. When Ty Spurlock invited us to BC to find brides, I made it clear that was for everyone but me. I made a deal, in fact, with Cosette that she leave me out of any sprinklings from her magic wand." He mopped his brow with a blue bandanna. "I'm everybody's friend and nobody's fellow, you see what I mean?"

She shrugged. "All you have to do is keep your lips sealed very tightly, Sam. If I'm going to catch John, I don't need you bringing him back home when he thinks he needs to be free."

He gulped, his brown eyes rolling nervously. "I don't want to agree to this, but I've seen the BC magic at work, and it's *potent* stuff."

"When applied correctly, yes, it is. Don't think for one minute that I couldn't convince Cosette that you're just talking big, Sam Barr, and like every other man claiming you don't want a woman. It wouldn't be hard to convince Cosette that settling the mischief-maker of

BC down would be a pièce de résistance for her magic wand."

He took a deep, shuddering breath. "Excuse me," he said, and got out of the truck. Reached into the double cab to pull a handful of ice from the cooler, wrapped it inside his blue bandanna and stuck it against his forehead. "He's going to know, Daisy. Someone will tell him."

"I'll cross that bridge when I come to it. But he can't know, not yet. He will know eventually," Daisy said. "You're going to have to give me time."

He nodded. "I know. I get it. I totally understand. You don't know John like I do, and he's superstitious as hell. You learn these things about a man in a war zone."

"Superstitious?"

"Yeah. He really bought into all that BC charm and nonsense."

"Nonsense!" Daisy sat up. "BC makes its living on that nonsense, and though I may be late to understanding it, I certainly endorse anything that fiscally benefits our town!"

Sam got back in the front seat, handing her a water bottle and cracking one open for himself. "Whatever happened up in Montana really changed you, Daisy. I don't know what potion Branch Winters poured over you, but it's a humdinger."

Daisy shook her head. "I fell in love," she said softly. "Branch helped me see the path, but the fact is, I've been in love with John for a long time. I was much too invested in my own pride to see it. And now I'm going to have to earn his, and the town's, trust. I'm willing to do that, but it's going to take time, which I won't have if you go bumping your gums all over BC."

"They'll know as soon as you start showing." He cast an aggrieved glance at her tummy.

"I have time." At least she hoped so.

Sam shook his head, glanced up at the roof of the truck. "Daisy Donovan, I'm only going to say this once because my whole body is going to go into shock, but there's only one way to bring my buddy back home, and to his senses, even."

"I'll happily take any advice you can give me." She meant every word, too. Earning John's trust wasn't going to be easy—she'd made quite a mess of things, and Daisy didn't need Sam, or Cosette or anybody else in town to spell that out for her.

"You're going to have to let me put a ring on your finger," Sam said, before passing out and falling over like a giant bear with its cotton stuffing pulled out.

She patted his face urgently. "Sam! Don't be a schmuck, I'm not marrying you!" Grabbing the cold bandanna, she wiped it over his face, shrieking when John knocked on the driver's-side window.

"John!"

He pulled open the door. "What the hell is going on?"

"Sam fainted!" She patted his face some more, willing color back into the dark skin. "He proposed to me, and then he—"

"What?" John helped her lay Sam across the seat and Daisy got out of the truck to make room. She worked on Sam at one end of the cab, and John worked on Sam from the driver's side. "You're gone five minutes and work a proposal out of Handsome Sam? Wake up, buddy," he said, touching cold water to Sam's face, "so I can knock you back out again!"

SAM CAME TO—finally!—and John breathed a sigh of relief. "Helluva a beauty nap you took there, buddy."

"What can I say? I need my forty winks." Sam sat up, glanced over at Daisy, whose face looked tragically concerned for Sam. "But I'm doing fine. This sexy, amazing woman has just agreed to—"

"Yeah, yeah." John helped his friend none too gently to sit up. "You big faker."

"Faker!" Sam looked outraged, any trace of the fallout he'd had gone for good. "I'm not faking anything!"

"Oh, you're a faker all right." John glared at the man whose back he'd had in Afghanistan, and vice versa. "Yelling at the top of your lungs that you want nothing to do with marriage, and the second I turn my back, you go and get—"

"What does your back have to do with anything?" Sam demanded.

"I'd like to know that myself." Daisy's concern turned to annoyance. "And what are you doing here, anyway? Last I saw you, you were heading north."

"I am heading north." He could barely meet Daisy's gaze. The truth was, his good sense had evaporated once he'd realized he was an epic dunce for letting her get away. He'd hopped into his truck and followed, not sure why, his heart driving him like a mad man. "You shouldn't have to drive all the way back to Bridesmaids Creek with Handsome Sam here. The least I can do is offer to fly you back. However, I had no idea that you and Sam—"

"Yep," Sam said, coming out of his coma ever more strongly by the second. He thumped his chest with pride. "Offer me the cup of congratulations, old buddy, old pal, I'm getting married."

"So you claimed."

John glanced at Daisy, but she didn't deny Sam's astonishing brag. Everyone knew that Sam was the last man on earth—the very last of any tribe, clan, or nationality—who would ever marry. Daisy gazed at him steadily, not appearing to be preparing to open her sumptuous, delightful lips for any sort of rebuttal, and John's heart fell to the ground, rolled around in the dust of the parking lot, then gave up the ghost.

"In fact, I'm having a baby," Sam said cheerfully, and the ghost of John's heart not only gave up, it poofed into nothingness. He felt cold all over, then hot, then drained. "*We're* having a baby."

"A baby?"

"It appears I'm going to be a father." Sam shook his head. "An astonishing thing, no?"

"Very." John raised a brow. "Let me get this straight. Daisy came after me, but you wanted her for yourself, and so you offered to drive her—"

"Just so." Sam nodded. John glanced to Daisy, who merely shrugged.

He stepped back from his friend, trying to piece all this together. Everyone knew Sam was a trickster beyond compare—if Shakespeare had still been alive, he could have written plays about this wizard of wackiness—but marriage? A baby?

John shook his head. "You two are fibbing through your teeth, but I'm darned if I know why."

Daisy didn't say anything, and Sam kept very still, like he was one breath short of hyperventilating again. John sighed. "Are you really this fickle? Or are you trying to make a point? Because I wouldn't put it past either one of you."

"What difference does it make to you?" Daisy asked.

"None." It meant every difference. He'd waited years for Daisy to come to her senses and realize he was the man of her dreams. Then, when she had come to her senses, he'd lost every one of his, apparently. Maybe lust had fried his brain. "Anyway, if you're content to ride home with my loose-marbled friend here, that's fine. I just wanted you to know that you could go by plane, too."

"You couldn't call to make your generous offer?" Daisy looked at him, and he thought she wasn't buying his cover story.

"I could have, but it seemed best to inquire in person." He looked at Sam. "My friend here means a lot to me. I know he was trying to do me a favor by bringing you after me."

"Really?" Daisy put a hand on a slim hip. "A favor? Does Sam truck women after you often, then?"

"Not at all. Which is why I felt the occasion merited the personal treatment."

"Well, thank you *so* much."

Daisy didn't sound very grateful. In fact, he thought he'd detected a tiny undertone of snark. He looked at her. "A baby? You two expect me to buy that you're having a baby?" He cast a gaze at her very flat stomach, with which he was intimately familiar, having spent hours kissing that very toned, very delectable flesh. "Something's off about this whole story."

It was indeed off. He'd used condoms with Daisy. She'd been very fine with that, in fact, one might even have said helpful, a foreplay which had stretched his manly capabilities to the max. John practically got stiff thinking about it. "A baby," he repeated. "I just don't think you have it in you, old man."

"What?" Sam squawked, sitting straight up with indignation. "I think I can handle parenthood just fine, thanks."

John shook his head. There was an alternate reality in here, he knew there was, but these two were thick as thieves about something. He looked at both of them, and then it hit him: his buddy was attempting to paint a bull's-eye on him with one of his infamous pranks.

Yes, Handsome Sam Barr was trying to pull a fast one.

And the only way to neutralize having a bull's-eye painted on one's hindquarters was to pull a faster one.

"You know," John said, "as I recall, Vegas is only a couple hours from here. Probably quite doable as a wedding destination in one day, considering how you like to apply your boot to the pedal."

Sam nodded vigorously. "We should be able to make it by nightfall for a romantic destination."

John looked at Daisy. "I wish you two well."

Daisy nodded, but she seemed uncertain. "Thank you."

"All right, then." Taking a deep breath, John got into the double cab, seating himself behind Sam and Daisy, and belted himself in with a grin.

Chapter Four

"What are you doing?" Daisy turned to meet John's mischievous gaze.

"I'm riding with you to Vegas." He put his hands behind his head, looking very comfortable and even pleased with himself.

Daisy frowned. "Why?"

He clapped Sam on the shoulder. "I can't let my buddy get married without a best man. And I *am* the best man. You may not know this about Sam and me, but we've seen some very dark days. Together, we survived."

Daisy glanced at Sam. He shrugged, and she thought she saw a little *what-can-we-do?* in his expressive eyes.

"We *are* best friends," Sam said.

Daisy turned to stare out the window. "I don't care."

"You don't mind if he tags along?" Sam asked.

"Hey! I prefer to think of myself less as a tagalonger and more as part of the wedding party."

Daisy didn't turn to look at John to sanction this silly statement. She was well aware he was taking Sam's role of being a trickster, but she wasn't going to be the one to cry "uncle." If these two wanted to play chicken, it was probably a game they'd played before. "I don't care one bit."

Sam turned to glare at John. "You can't cause any trouble."

"Me?" John feigned surprise and innocence. "I never cause trouble."

"Never cause trouble," Sam muttered under his breath, starting the truck, and Daisy wondered how this situation was going to end up by nightfall. John appeared determined to call Sam's bluff, so there was a great possibility that Sam might find himself at the altar saying "I do," something he'd always proclaimed he would never do.

Until today.

This was terrible. With John sitting in the backseat goading his friend on, Sam might not feel as if he could bow out. Sam had just been trying to bring John to his senses—but like other plans in Bridesmaids Creek had been known to go, this one appeared to have taken a turn for the worse.

I don't even need anyone to marry me.

With the two men dug in for the long haul, apparently, Daisy decided she might as well take a nap. Pretend to take one, anyway—as if she could ignore John's long, lean body in the backseat. She could feel his gaze on her, studying her. Waiting to see if she'd crack.

The man really believed she was so hung up on him that he could haul out of town without saying goodbye—then show back up in her life and throw the equivalent of a cold, wet water balloon to explode her plans.

Ass.

"I'm sorry, pumpkin, did you say something?" Sam asked, clearly intending to play the *This Is Chicken and*

I'm Not Gonna Lose scenario to its incongruous end. "It sounded like you said *ass*."

Daisy shook her head, kept her eyes closed. "I didn't say ass."

"I thought I heard her say ass," John said, putting his two cents in from the backseat.

"Guys, leave me out of the rooster-like posturing, please," she said, and they had the nerve to guffaw.

"Daisy, lady, you're far too much for my gentle friend to handle," John said.

"And yet he's handling me just fine," Daisy said, and that shut John up for the space of five blissful minutes.

Of course, John had to start fielding calls on his cell phone. From the backseat, she could hear him gossiping about today's wedding plans. He told everyone who called that she and Sam were running off—which of course brought on a flurry of phone calls, all of which John seemed pleased to discuss in laborious detail. Daisy's nerves were stretched tight, and Sam looked positively unlike himself.

Handsome Sam had turned into a shadow of his former devil-may-care self.

Daisy was relieved when Sam finally pulled up in Vegas. He'd found a quaint little chapel, a white incongruous place that didn't shout Elvis.

"I'll take the groom in and tidy him up," John said jovially, and Daisy snapped, "Fine."

"Ooh, bridal nerves," John whispered to Sam, but he made sure his whisper carried. "I think she's got 'em bad!"

She was going to clock John Lopez Mathison a good one if he didn't take his annoying self far from her. A delicate, elderly woman approached. "You must be the bride."

"Not today," Daisy said. "I'll give you five hundred dollars if you sneak me out of here and keep those two hunky cowboys I came in with busy long enough for me to get to the nearest airport."

KNOWING THE FIRST place Sam and John would look for her was Bridesmaids Creek or Branch Winters's place in Montana, Daisy took herself somewhere she knew she was totally safe. She went to New York, waited a day for her father to overnight her passport, and flew out to Australia, where Robert Donovan had recently purchased properties. It was a great excuse to check out the real estate, which made her father happy, but most of all, it gave Daisy time to think through her situation.

For a girl who loved riding fast on her motorcycle, her life had become way too fast-paced. She was going to be a mother. It was time to sit and think, figure out what she was going to do. Here she was completely safe from the game-playing duo of John and Sam.

She put a hand on her stomach as she looked out over the Sydney skyline. John had never suspected the baby was his—which had annoyed the heck out of her, but they'd been completely faithful about using condoms, so she guessed she could understand why he might assume the baby was Sam's.

Then again, he was still an ass. She might have been wild, but she'd never been promiscuous, and John knew that. Part of her wondered if Sam would tell him the truth—but one never knew with Sam. He marched to the beat of his own unseen drummer, one that played a tune no one could predict.

It would all work out. She had to believe that. To think otherwise would mean giving up on the BC magic—something she would never do. Her father owned buildings around the world; she could live anywhere she liked. But Bridesmaids Creek was home.

And that's where her baby would be born.

She just needed to let the smoke clear. Once John and Sam cooled their jets, she'd return.

It was time to make up for her part in the problems in BC—and she'd never been a girl to back down from what she knew had to be done.

She couldn't wait to get started.

"THAT'S THE FUNNIEST story I ever heard!" Sheriff Dennis slapped his thigh, causing the biggest frown he could muster to crease John's face. Cosette Lafleur and Jane Chatham didn't appear to be any less amused by the tale of Daisy ditching both him and Sam at the altar, so this was just one more BC legend John was going to have to live down.

He didn't mind admitting that he didn't understand Daisy. He prided himself on being able to catch anything that moved on the planet—anything. He'd been an excellent sniper—hence Squint, short for Squint-Eye—he'd been proud to protect his fellow countrymen. He had no trouble bagging any kind of game, and horseshoes and hand grenades were right up his tree of fun.

But the sexy brunette with the key to his soul—she confounded him. Eluded him, and stunned him. He'd had every intention of making her go all the way up to the altar with Sam, for the sheer pleasure of watching her back out at the last second.

Oh, she'd backed out big-time. They were lucky she hadn't taken the truck and stranded them in Sin City.

One day he'd have to thank her for not doing that. He couldn't really have blamed her if she had.

The worst part was nobody knew where she'd gone—or if they did, they sure as heck weren't telling. John sent a sour look to his booth mates at The Wedding Diner.

"One of you has to know something. She couldn't have just disappeared."

The three haphazard matchmakers shook their collective heads in the negative.

"You won't find her, wherever she went," Cosette said. "Robert's got ventures all around the world. Last I heard, he'd bought up something in Shanghai." She frowned. "Or maybe it was Bangkok."

John tipped his hat back. "It's all my fault, anyway. If she wants peace and quiet, she should get all she wants."

"Your fault?" Dennis asked.

"Yeah. I pushed her." He sighed. "Sam's mad as the dickens at me, too. He said I was being a louse, and that he was doing his very best to get me moving."

"To be fair, Daisy never gave you a whole lot of encouragement until lately."

"I wish I could use that as an excuse, but I can't." Since she'd seduced him in Montana—or had he seduced her?—it had all happened so fast and seemed so beneficially organic.

"It's funny how we used to call her the Diva of Destruction." Sheriff Dennis laughed. "That seems a long time ago now."

Daisy was still a diva to him—the Diva of Delights. They couldn't understand how mad he was about her, had been from the moment he'd laid eyes on her zooming around on her motorcycle.

"Patience has never been a virtue of mine."

They laughed. "Nor ours," Cosette said.

"In the meantime," Jane said, "you can be our fall guy. Just until Daisy gets back. She will come back one day, you know."

"Fall guy?" He perked up. This sounded distinctly dangerous. One didn't sign up to be a fall guy in Bridesmaids Creek willy-nilly. This crew could think up some wingdingers.

Jane nodded. "We need you to find out whose baby Daisy is having. We must be prepared."

The blood left John's head. "Whose baby?" He couldn't bear thinking about it. "I thought they were just making up that tale."

The ladies looked at him, concerned. "Daisy's really expecting," Jane said.

He sat dumbfounded, shell-shocked.

After a moment, Jane sighed and went on. "Well, it's clear Daisy thinks she's going to do this all on her own. She's just that kind of independent woman. Goodness knows she doesn't need a man for financial reasons." Jane shook her head. "If that's not your baby—"

"I'm afraid not." His ears were ringing, to go with the light-headedness assailing him. He couldn't bear to think of Daisy even kissing another man, much less having a baby! "Do you have anything stronger than tea, Jane?"

The three gentle folk looked at him with grave concern.

"I keep some whiskey in the back for after hours," Jane whispered. "On occasion, our close-knit group likes to sit in one of the circular booths and enjoy a small tipple."

"I could use a small tipple." John couldn't imagine Daisy being held in another man's arms. Oh, Sam had tried to make him jealous, but no one was jealous of Handsome Sam.

But he hadn't thought through the fact that Daisy might be with child by another man.

"We're wondering if Branch Winters did more than reroute Daisy's brain," Dennis said, and cold and hot swamped John in nauseating waves. "Something happened up there, something big."

"He changed her," Cosette said. "We're wondering if perhaps Daisy might have fallen for—"

"I can't," John said. He leaned back in the booth, and when Jane put the "tipple" in front of him in a sweetly painted tea cup to disguise its contents from the other patrons, John knocked it back without hesitation.

"Easy there, sailor," Dennis said. "It'll be closing time soon. I'll take you to my place and we'll cauterize your brain for a bit. Or maybe Phillipe's place for some yoga. I'm really getting into that yoga crap Phillipe's got going on, Cosette. Do you do it?"

"I do, and I'm getting so flexible! Who would have ever thought my husband would become a yogi of sorts?" Cosette looked pleased, and John noticed that she didn't refer to Phillipe as her ex-husband. Maybe matters were looking up for them. He sure hoped so.

"I'll pass on the yoga." After their divorce, Phillipe had moved into a small house, and outfitted it with hanging beads and floor cushions for the yoga practice he'd started. It looked like a regular hangout for hippies, which had caught them all off guard because Phillipe and Cosette were anything but the hippie type.

Cosette picked up the delicate floral teapot and poured some more amber liquid into his cup. "You look like you could use another smidge of whiskey."

"And all this time I thought you sat in this booth and drank tea." John shook his head.

"We do!" Jane glanced at her friends. "But on occasion, like right now, something with a little oomph is required. Now, if you're feeling fortified, let's get back to the topic at hand, which is Daisy."

He froze up again. "I can't be the fall guy. I can't even think about it." He swallowed hard. "Anyway, isn't it her business who the father of her child might be?"

"Maybe," Dennis said, "unless the father lives in Montana or something."

Crap. He could see where they were going with this. Daisy Donovan might just have allowed herself, in a moment of heartbreak and confusion, to be seduced. The cold chills he'd suffered a moment ago came back with a vengeance, despite the whiskey he'd quaffed out of the eggshell-thin teacup.

She might not ever return to Bridesmaids Creek.

"I suppose you're absolutely certain, one hundred percent sure that the baby couldn't possibly be yours... not that we're trying to pry?" Jane asked gently.

He read between those lines. "Oh, you're dying to pry, but I know you mean well." He took a long, deep breath. "I suppose the way things work in BC, I can't entirely count out the remote, infinitesimal poss—"

"I knew it!" Cosette clapped her hands.

Jane beamed. She made another pour out of the teapot for the entire table, making sure John's went clean to the rim of his cup. "This calls for a celebration!"

"Now wait," John said. "I was going to say that Daisy's baby being mine would be something on the order of a miraculous—"

They all looked at him, their faces gleaming as his words drifted away. Each of them looked so pleased he couldn't bear to let them down.

"You have to understand, you'd be better off looking for another bachelor," John said. "I'm not your man."

"He may be right," Jane said thoughtfully. "I don't know that I'm feeling it."

Dennis wore the same suddenly thoughtful look. "And then there's the matter of Sam. I still can't figure out how he got into this."

John didn't want to hear about Handsome Sam. "Trust me, my buddy was just trying to help me get to the altar. It was all an elaborate sham to coax me there."

"Most men don't offer to marry a woman who's having a child that isn't theirs." Cosette grew pensive now, too. "I mean, *you're* not."

His throat got a bit tight. "I haven't really thought about—"

"The thing about Sam," Dennis said, "is that he really is an ultimate bachelor with a golden heart. Someone should hook him."

John shook his head. "You'll never catch Sam."

"But he was taking her to Vegas," Jane said. "That gives me pause about this bachelor song he sings."

A little doubt crept into John. "Sam's just up to his usual tricks. We all suffer from it. And love him for it, too," he said truthfully.

"Well," Cosette said brightly, "I suppose it doesn't

matter whether you're in love with Daisy. She's not here, and who knows when she'll come home after the shock she's suffered."

"Wait a minute." John's brain whirred like a pinwheel. Which fallacy should he start with—that he was in love with Daisy, or that she might never return? This was BC: she *had* to return. "I'm not in love with Daisy."

The second the words left his mouth, causing glints of mirth and knowing to shine in his friends' eyes, John knew—just as they knew—that he was head over heels, gone-and-not-coming-back, certifiably in love with Daisy Donovan.

"Oh, crap," he said, and they high-fived each other, and then him, for good measure.

This was a problem. He was now squarely in BC's sights, and the worst part was, he had no clue where Daisy was, and if that was his child she was carrying.

Holy smoke.

Chapter Five

"And that's that," John told Daisy's gang. "You lot are going to help me make this right. And if that's not high irony, I don't know what is."

Daisy's gang of five, seated in their new man cave, shook their lunkheads. "We can't help you," Dig said.

"No aid to the enemy," Red said.

"She's our girl," Clint said, "even if she didn't choose one of us."

"We don't see what a great girl like her would see in a squid like you," Carson said.

"And we haven't given up hope," Gabriel said. "We're not helping any Handsome Sams, Squints or Frogs. Where do you guys get these names, anyway?"

So he was sitting square in enemy camp, with conspirators unwilling to be his wingmen in his hunt to find Daisy. "Listen, Daisy's having a baby, and she's going to need our help."

"*Our* help," Red said. "Not necessarily *your* help."

"Unless you're the father," Carson said, "and we don't see that being the case."

John shrugged. "Of course I'm the father. Who else do you think it would be?" Here he was fibbing just a bit because he didn't know for sure, but in the night, he'd ruminated over what his friends had said to him at The Wedding Diner and realized it really didn't matter who the father of Daisy's baby was. He was in love with her, and he'd be a good father, a dad to her child.

As far as John was concerned, that made it case closed for his suit.

They glared at him, not believing him.

"Daisy would have told us," Clint said. "We've got our money on it being that fellow up in Montana. The airy-fairy one who lives in the wild and communes with nature and all that crapola."

John laughed. "Branch would get a real charge out of hearing himself described that way."

"So?" Carson demanded. "How do you know Daisy's not with him?"

"Because she's not. And we need to find her, fellows."

"Again," Dig said, "*we* need to find her. There's no you and us in this situation. *We've* known her since she was three years old, and *we* don't need any outside help rescuing her from what was clearly an unfortunate decision on her part."

"That's too bad." John leaned back in one of the leather chairs, glanced around the man cave. "It'd be good for your new business to showcase your first success as date makers."

"You're not one of our clients," Red said.

"Because you don't have any yet," John said, pointing out the obvious. "If you're going to be the premier dating service and cigar bar," he said, glancing with doubt toward the leather-wrapped cigar bar and wooden walls that shouted man cave, in complete opposition to the idea of being a dating service, "you need a high-profile client to highlight what you can do. And that's me."

They gawked at him. John could hear the wheels turning.

"He's right," Clint said reluctantly.

"Never say that an out-of-towner is right," Carson said, his words hushed.

"Nevertheless, he has a point," Dig said, his voice stunned.

"At least it's not Handsome Sam," Gabriel said. "I think I can stand anything but giving our girl up to a man with a handle like that!"

THE SIX MEN got out of the two trucks, warily eyeing the Donovan compound.

"Well," Dig said to John as they stared at the massive two-story gray edifice, "here's the yellow brick road. And while you might want us to play your Cowardly Lion, Tin Man, Scarecrow, Toto and—"

"I'm not playing Dorothy," Red said, "no cracks about my hair or anything."

They gazed at his long red mop for a second. John didn't think there was a man on earth he'd rather deem Dorothy less than Red. The man had arm muscles that looked like a bear's.

"Cowardly Lion, Tin Man, Scarecrow, Toto and a flying monkey," Dig said, his tone impatient with his friend.

"Okay, I can go with a flying monkey. They were kind of cool," Red said, but they ignored him and went back to staring at the house where Daisy lived, and thus, her warlock of a father.

John shook his head. "I really don't know if this is the right plan, fellows."

"Well, you came to us for help, need I remind you?" Carson said. "And this is how we suggest you help yourself. You're going to have to man up and ask for his daughter's hand in marriage."

"What?" John said, and Daisy's gang favored him with narrow gazes.

"That's what we're here for, isn't it?" Gabriel demanded.

"I was going to start small," John said, "like maybe let Robert Donovan know that I'd like to find his daughter."

They shook their heads.

"Here's the problem," Clint said. "We have it on good authority that Donovan doesn't know his little angel is expecting his grandchild."

"That can't be possible. This is BC," John said. "Everybody knows everything about everybody, and if they don't, it's because they've buried themselves deep under a rock."

"And just who do you think would tell Mr. Donovan that his daughter is in the family way?" Dig asked, staring at him. "Don't you think he'd have had a word or two with the man he thought had knocked up his daughter and left her high and dry?"

"You being that fellow and all," Red said, "now that the truth has come out."

"No truth has come out!" John said, but he was beginning to wonder himself. He'd asked Sam, but Sam had denied knowing who the father of Daisy's baby was. Swore up and down that he didn't care, either. If

Daisy needed a husband, then Sam Barr was more than happy to be that husband.

Jealousy had practically eaten a hole in John's cool, calm persona—and Sam knew it. Enjoyed it, even.

"But admit it, you're beginning to think you're going to be shopping for blue or pink in the very near future," Clint said, and John's breath hitched.

"It's actually a pretty appealing idea," he said, and they clapped him on the back in the nearest sign of camaraderie he'd experienced from them. "Hey! You're trying to get me to go up there, spill the beans—which are Daisy's beans to spill, by the way—and get my head pounded down my neck!"

They guffawed, just a bunch of knuckleheads having a great day, more than happy to add him to their group for the moment because it made them a whole half-dozen cars on the crazy train for a change.

"Aw, Donovan's not going to pound your head," Dig said. "Nobody's afraid of Daddy Warbucks anymore. But you *are* going to get the speech about how you're not worthy of his adorable daughter, and how he ought to bury you under Best Man's Fork where no one can find your remains for knocking up his baby girl, and that if you think you're going to get one penny of his dough you're crazier than a bedbug."

"Well, when you put it that way, how can I resist?" John asked, not that worried about Donovan, anyway. A security truck pulled up, with Donovan riding shotgun to see who was trespassing on his holy land, and the five dummkopfs scattered in their truck.

"What brings you to my humble abode, Squint?" Donovan demanded as the dust plume rose from John's newfound friends' hauling asses.

"It's John now, Robert. And I'd like a moment of your time," John said, and the man narrowed his eyes at him.

It wasn't a stare most people would like to receive, but John had seen a lot worse. He shrugged. "If you have time, that is. Sir."

Just like his military days, he knew when to apply the courtesy treatment. Robert perked up.

"I might spare you five minutes. Start talking."

"Actually, what I've come to say is private." John glanced at the armed guards and the driver, who was no doubt packing as well, with a shrug. "Regarding family business."

Robert grumbled a bit. "I suppose you want to be invited in."

John shrugged again.

"Those five wienies who just hit the road have never darkened the doors of my house. Why would I let you in?"

"I can talk out in the fresh air just as well as inside four walls, Robert. I'm just asking for you to hear me out in private."

After a moment, Robert got out. His men drove away. "So, you've come to find out where my daughter is. She said you would."

"I'm glad she knows me so well."

"Harrumph!"

"Look, Robert, I happen to think an awful lot of your daughter, and——"

"Son, let me stop you." Robert drew himself up to his full six feet four and glared. "I know where you come from, I know about your family. What do you imagine you can possibly offer my daughter?"

John ignored that, took a deep breath and then the

plunge. "There's a very good chance Daisy may be having my baby. I need to find her."

Robert shook his head gravely. "My daughter isn't expecting a child. Not yours, or anybody else's. Someone's been blowing smoke in your face, in order to get you to make this ill-advised journey. And it *was* ill-advised."

John shrugged. "Regardless, I need to find Daisy. I'd like to talk to her."

"My daughter has asked me not to reveal her whereabouts. Says she'll come home when she's ready." Robert shook his head at John. "I'll honor Daisy's wishes."

Robert turned to leave.

"One more thing, sir."

Robert turned again. "I appreciate that Daisy needs some time to herself." He met Robert's eyes with determination. "Just know that when she does return to BC, I will be asking for her hand in marriage."

"You'll never get a penny of mine," Robert warned.

"I don't recall asking for any of your money," John said. He eyed the great gray house behind them. "Honestly, your way of life wouldn't suit me at all. I'm used to something far different. And just know that Daisy, should she accept my suit, would always be taken care of in every way."

"Your parents are itinerant rodeo workers!" Robert sputtered.

John nodded. "That's right. Good people, too. Daisy and I would do just fine on my earnings as a rodeo worker. Don't count your daughter out, Robert. She's tougher than you think she is."

He got into his truck and departed, feeling really good about the way the conversation had gone.

Daisy's gang was waiting for him at the end of the drive, around the corner and well out of eyeshot of the main house. John pulled over, and got out to join them.

They stared at him, agog.

"It was brave of you to hang around, but I told you everything would be fine." John waited for the onslaught of questions, which began almost as soon as his words left his mouth.

"Are you getting married?"

"Did he know Daisy's pregnant?"

"Where's our Daisy?"

"Fellows, fellows." He held up a hand to stem the cacophony. "I said everything was fine. I didn't say that Robert had given away any information. I know nothing more than when you last saw me. However, Donovan now knows of my intent to marry his daughter, so that puts a new wrinkle in the dynamic of everybody's favorite busybodying small town."

He tipped his hat to them, and got back into his truck. With a jaunty wave, he drove away, not giving away that he had no idea what he was going to do next.

JOHN SETTLED INTO bed at the bunkhouse, placing himself on his back, one arm behind his head so he could lie still and stare at the ceiling. Not that he could see the ceiling in the dark, but stare he did, deep in thought.

His mind was turned inside out; he hardly knew what to believe. BC claimed Daisy was having a baby; no one knew whose.

Robert Donovan said she wasn't, and that his daughter merely needed to be left alone.

Someone wasn't telling the truth, and if John had to guess, he'd say none of them was telling the unvarnished truth. Oh, there were probably bits and pieces of truth scattered in and out of all the stories—but he was being steered, there was no question of that.

It was the way BC operated. Besides which, the only person who had all the information was Daisy—and she clearly intended to remain a silent party.

Very unusual for her, too.

The door opened. Someone came in, closed it behind them.

"Hello?" John waited, holding back a yawn. More than likely Sam or one of the hands didn't realize he'd gotten back. Listening carefully, he knew he wasn't in danger.

Two people, both women.

"John!" Cosette's delicate French accent hissed in the darkness.

"You can turn a light on." He sat up, swung his legs over the bed, reached for his jeans, pulled them up.

"Are you decent?" Cosette asked.

"I am now." He waited, decided to flip the lamp on the bedside table to put his visitors out of their misery. "Hello, Jane, Cosette."

They solemnly nodded. He studied their clothes. Both women wore black, from their little feet to their necks, including long sleeves. They each had on a black hat. "Are we getting out our cauldron tonight, ladies?" he asked.

"Very funny." Jane waved an imperative hand at him. "Please dress yourself. We dare not linger. Someone will surely notice that you have visitors in your room."

"Surely they would notice, since I haven't had any female companionship in my room in, oh, since I've been employed at the Hanging H." Sighing, he stood, reaching for a white T-shirt with a Hanging H advertisement on the front. He happened to glance at the ladies, noted their raised eyebrows, tossed the white shirt away. "I take it you prefer more of the look of the cloak and dagger?"

Cosette gave him a narrow look. "A little less laughter, a little more action. I thought SEALs could get dressed in under sixty seconds or something? That they even sleep in their clothes?"

"Our SEAL appears to be more of the relaxed variety. And remember, he did come in dead last in the Bridesmaids Creek swim." Jane said this with a perfectly innocent face.

"I had a leg cramp!" John said for the hundredth time that story had been brought up. He pulled on a black T-shirt. "Shall I camouflage my face and get my night vision glasses?"

"Sarcasm," Jane whispered to Cosette. "Some men employ sarcasm when they feel nervous or inadequate."

John grunted, recognizing he was being needled. "I assure you, I am neither. However, I am wondering why you've crept into my bedroom in the middle of the night dressed like munchkin witches escaped from the Haunted H."

"A laugh a minute," Cosette said.

"A regular riot," Jane agreed. "Let's go."

They sneaked him out the back, making certain not to alert any of the other bunkhouse inhabitants to their presence. Once outside, they shooed him into a waiting truck, driven by Sheriff Dennis.

"Really? You let them talk you into this kind of midnight debauchery?" John demanded, getting into the back.

"Just settle in, son. We have a lot of work to do."

John buckled up. The ladies piled in the front next to their getaway driver, and the truck disappeared into the night. "I guess you realize that if something happens to me, if you're planning to hide my body in a secret location, no one will know it was you who talked me out of my comfy bed. You'll be free and clear from public suspicion."

"Again, he's just stocked with knee-slappers," Jane said.

"Your audience is rolling in the aisles," Cosette chimed in.

John decided to sit quietly and just wait for his friends to get their practical joke out of their systems. They were so serious, completely unlike their normally lighthearted selves, that he caught the mood and settled back for the ride.

Fifteen minutes later, he judged they were near the creek. He refrained from inquiring whether they were planning to drown him, which would go over like a lead balloon with them in their current disposition. They got out, and he noted Dennis had hidden the truck behind a stand of trees.

He had a very strange feeling about these late-night fun and games, but he followed the trio obediently.

"Did I tell you I had a chat with Robert Donovan?" he asked, and they automatically shushed him.

That was the biggest piece of news he had, and if they weren't interested in that, he was literally just a fourth wheel on their nocturnal excursion. Cosette and Jane went behind some trees, and suddenly, they disappeared. John stopped, waiting, glancing at Dennis, who pointed to a rock wall.

"Go," the sheriff said.

John didn't move. "What about you?"

"I'm the lookout. In case you don't come out."

"That makes me feel better," John said drily, but suddenly, a small feminine hand grabbed his, jerking him behind the rock and down a long incline that seemed to go on and on forever. John had new respect for Cosette's and Jane's ability to power walk, allowing himself to be dragged deeper into the cavern. Clearly this was a secret kept from the general public, and probably known only to these three stalwarts of Bridesmaids Creek. He figured they were a good bit under the creek now, far deeper than he cared to be subterranean with only the ladies' flashlights to light the way.

Suddenly a room appeared, grand in scope and design. He stayed very still as the ladies lit torches on the walls, revealing a place so hauntingly beautiful it might have been spun by prehistoric fairies. "Holy Christmas."

"Indeed." Cosette gazed at the room. "You are now in the presence of the secret of Bridesmaids Creek."

Chapter Six

"Well, this is *one* of the secrets of Bridesmaids Creek," Jane clarified. "This cave was discovered by my great-great-great-grandmother, Eliza Chatham, who was the original founder of our town. This secret has been passed down in my family, and I've shared it with only the people here tonight."

"I'm honored."

"You should be." Cosette looked around the room. "This place has withstood every kind of weather condition imaginable. Never flooded, never cracked from a tremor. It's clearly a marvel of engineering."

"Who built it?" John looked at the medieval decor with some fascination.

"We're not sure. There were Native Americans in this area at the time, but some of the carvings appear more French or Spanish in nature." The ladies seated themselves at a carved rock table, pulled a box from a hiding place in the center of it.

"Why are you showing this to me? I'm not a son of BC."

"No," Jane said, "but would we trust this knowledge to Daisy's gang?"

"Why trust it to anyone?"

They gazed at him, their faces sincere in the lamplight. "It's time to pass the knowledge on. We chose you," Cosette said, "to be the guardian."

"Why?" He found this hard to believe. He wasn't a true son of BC, not the way Ty Spurlock was. "Why not Mackenzie or Suz or Jade?"

They considered him, as if he were slow on the uptake.

"The magic is here," Jane said. "And you need the magic more than most."

That was probably an understatement. "You're feeling sorry for me because I never got the girl. In fact, the girl in question barely looked my way for years." He shrugged. "Thanks, ladies, but I'm not sure there's enough magic in BC to get that one to the altar. At least not with me."

"What did you and Robert discuss?" Cosette asked.

"Daisy." Just saying her name made him happy, then gave him a sense of despair. "He wouldn't tell me where she is. Says she doesn't want to be found."

"All right. Focus," Jane said, placing the box in the middle of the table. "We're going to figure out the best way to get Daisy back."

"How are we going to do that?"

"We're going to talk about it," Cosette said, her tone perplexed. "Did you think we have a crystal ball?"

John laughed. "I wouldn't put it past you."

They stared at him in bemusement.

"Sometimes I wonder about this younger generation," Jane said. "No seriousness at all."

He forbore to say that, at times, both these ladies had been known to have their humorous and maybe even irreverent moments.

"We put a private eye on Daisy," Cosette said. "Not to spy on her, just to locate her, you understand."

He leaned back. "I don't think that's quite the way I want to locate Daisy. It might be creeper-like, if you ask me."

Jane sniffed. "Okay, we have one handsome prince who doesn't care to travel to Australia."

"Australia! Are you serious?"

They peered at him, their faces concerned.

"Okay, okay," he said. "I get it. This is a serious night. Poor choice of words."

"Yes," Cosette said sourly. "Now, then, what are you going to do about it?"

"Look, why don't I just do the simple thing and call her?" John thought that sounded reasonable.

"How do you know she'd answer?" Jane asked.

"Why wouldn't she? She's not angry with me. She's just—" John told himself to slow down, not let the ladies stir him up. "Daisy's on an important mission to find herself."

"With a baby," Cosette said.

"Maybe *your* baby," Jane said. "Does that add up to you?"

He felt a cold splash of reality hit him. "Why are you two so positive she's having my baby?"

Jane looked reluctant to spill, but then the dam burst. "Because Daisy was taking the same medication Suz and Mackenzie and Jade Harper were taking, to boost their chances of pregnancy. We know you spent time together in Montana. Before you, Daisy had never had a—"

He looked at them. "Never had a what?"

"A real man," Cosette said, and he coughed.

"*Any* man," Jane said. "She's never, ever had a boyfriend, even. Robert was far too protective for silly boys hanging around his princess, you may be sure. In fact, we always thought Daisy's gang were handpicked plants. Robert knew every one of those five guys were no threat to his princess, his baby girl. Or his kingdom. They didn't have the firepower nor the candlepower to warm Daisy's heart."

The cold splash turned positively glacial, chilling him. It wasn't possible. Daisy Donovan couldn't have been a virgin. He would have known—wouldn't he?

He thought back, realizing that she had seemed a bit more heated the second and following times they'd made love. He'd put it down to the fact that she'd been shy the first time they'd made love. Not shy—a virgin.

The chill intensified. She'd been on the secret, super-duper ovary-booster of which Mackenzie, Suz and Jade had spoken of. All of those women had given birth to multiples. He wondered why Daisy would have needed—or wanted—to take a drug like that, couldn't focus on that for more than a second before he realized the implications: he could wind up a father of multiples—if Daisy was, as Cosette and Jane seemed to believe, pregnant from their very sexy interlude in Montana. "How do you know Daisy was on that medication?" John demanded.

"Suz told me. Daisy was hoping to have a baby one day, figured it would take a long time for the medicine to start working. I believe she started the medication right before she went to Montana." Cosette shrugged. "You could be in for a big shocker, John Lopez Mathison. You may not want to go to Australia, but you'd better figure out a way to get our hometown girl back home where she belongs!"

FIVE HOURS LATER, after coffee-klatching with the ladies until the crack of dawn, John rolled into the kitchen at the Hanging H with a new sense of purpose.

"Whoa," Justin Morant said, pouring fresh coffee into a mug, and adding another mug when he saw John's face. "Who pounded steel into your spine this morning?"

"I've had a revelation." John hesitated. "Hey, remember when you first came to Bridesmaids Creek?"

"I do, thanks to Ty Spurlock, it's burned in my mind forever." Justin laughed. "Best thing that ever happened to me."

"You love being a father to those four girls."

Justin nodded, grinning. "Those little ladies make my every day a reason for happiness. And, good news, just between you and me, Mackenzie is expecting another baby." His grin grew more huge. "Thankfully, this time it's a single."

"Congratulations." John high-fived Justin, raised his coffee cup. "If I can do as good a job as you are of being a father, I'll consider myself a success."

Justin looked at him, dug out a couple of slices of homemade cinnamon cake for both of them and slid a plate over to John. "So, Daisy's having your baby. You ready for fatherhood?"

"I wasn't yesterday." John shrugged. "But I figure you stepped up for Mackenzie and her four. I can handle one little baby." He sipped his coffee. "I hope."

Justin raised his mug. "I have faith. It's easier than it looks."

"Becoming a father to four doesn't look easy at all."

"You'd be surprised how much fun it is." Justin forked up a bite of his cake, chewed thoughtfully. "Those little ladies just wrap you around your finger, and the next thing you know, you're hooked like a prize fish."

John felt hooked, reeled in, and tossed into the boat freezer. "Hey, I'm thinking about taking a sabbatical."

Justin raised a brow. "To Australia?"

"How'd you know?"

Justin laughed. "It's all over the town grapevine. You're going to bring the hometown girl home."

"Yeah." John shook his head. "I'm not sure it's a good idea, but the sweet busybodies seem to think I should give it a shot. Personally, I feel I should give the lady in question some space."

"Too long apart can make her forget you ever made her happy."

"I don't want to think about that."

"And a little morning sickness can actually make her hate your guts, especially since she's suffering on her own." Justin laughed at the expression on John's face. "Well, it's just an idea. What do I know about love?"

John polished off his cake and headed out the door. It would take him two days' travel to get to Australia—and every second counted.

He was astonished to find Daisy Donovan sitting on her motorcycle, just like old times, wrapped in black moto wear and looking hotter than summer. "Hello," he said, too shocked to say more.

She gazed at him for a long moment. "Do you have a minute? There's something we should talk about."

The cold chill that had cast itself over him ever since his nocturnal kidnap by Cosette and Co. completely evaporated, to be replaced by a raging inferno of sexual desire. And a lot of other emotions, none of which he had time to dissect. "Sure. I'm good for a chat."

"Hop on." She jerked her head to indicate the portion of seat behind her, and John had never grabbed a helmet so fast in his life. He was on the bike in record time, carefully wrapping his hands around her waist, noticing a couple of inches that hadn't been there before. Actually, without letting his fingers wander, he very much detected quite a bit of a rounding tummy, maybe four inches worth.

John grinned to himself. He was going to be a father. At least he hoped so.

DAISY TOOK HIM to The Wedding Diner, which wasn't open yet due to the early morning hour, but Jane seemed to be expecting them. She ushered them in through the back door—apparently as expected. She seated them in a corner, away from prying eyes and ears, which seemed odd to John as there was no one there but Jane and a couple of kitchen helpers. Still, he wasn't going to complain about the location of the white vinyl booth since it meant he was almost virtually alone with the woman with whom he wanted to speak badly.

Jane set a teapot of hot water with its accompanying tea basket and a blue-checked cloth-lined basket of zucchini and pumpkin mini muffins in front of them, and then went to seat another group. Daisy poured hot water into both their cups, they selected some teas from the basket, and John waited with his heart hammering in his throat.

"When did you get back?" he asked, by way of icebreaker. It seemed like a safe topic, but then again, there was really no such thing in BC.

"Last night. My father said you wanted to see me."

"I didn't figure he'd tell you I went to rattle his cage a bit."

"Actually, he claimed you asked for my hand in marriage."

Now this seemed promising. John perked up. "In fact, I did."

Daisy gazed at him, no smile on her face, but a steady look that didn't speak of revulsion, either. He took that as a good sign and swiped a pumpkin muffin just to look like he was casual about the whole going-by-to-see-your-dad-and-asking-for-your-hand thing—which he most certainly was not.

"So?" Daisy said.

"So nothing. We had a bit of back and forth, and that was it." He saw no reason to go into more detail. "I felt it was a good conversation, with points of view presented on both sides."

Daisy sipped delicately from her teacup, her gaze locked on him over the rim. "Dad says he told you he'd rather have a village idiot for a son-in-law."

John laughed. "Your father talks big. And yet here you are, clearly open to my suit."

"You're pretty sure of yourself."

He grinned. "You're having my baby, aren't you?"

It wasn't a question; it was a bald statement of fact—the little ladies had convinced him that it could be no other way. Daisy was finally going to be his. He could hardly wait to shout it from the rooftops.

"I'm having your triplets," Daisy said, and the smile blew off John's face. His head spun. All he could do was stare at her in stunned silence.

Daisy put her cup down. "I didn't mean for that to happen, honestly."

"I think someone's telling a wee fib," John said. "Our dear friends tell me that you were on some kind of miracle ovary juice. That isn't the mark of a woman who doesn't want a man's child."

"I meant," Daisy said calmly, "that I didn't mean to have *your* child."

He raised a brow. "We did use condoms every time."

Condoms being plural, of course, which spoke to the truth, which was that each and every time he'd gotten his hands on this deliciously wild woman, he'd made the most of it.

There could have been some slippage. A misfire of eagerness, perhaps, with a condom not being appropriately placed. The thing was, Daisy's hands were so small, so feminine, so deft, that when she stroked him, helping with the condom, it was all he could do not to—

"The thing is," Daisy said, and John forced himself to focus on her lips and not the sweetest times, "it wasn't my intention to rope you into a wedding. And I'm afraid that's what you think, judging by the fact that you bearded the lion in his den."

"Your father's not much of a lion these days," John said absently. "Why did he tell you all this? And why didn't you tell me you were expecting in the first place, Daisy? Why'd you leave?"

"I left because it was crazy-town around here. I wasn't sure what I wanted to do."

"It's always crazy-town. You didn't expect BC to change, Daisy?"

"I didn't want you to feel compelled to marry me. I don't need a husband."

"And yet, you're going to have a husband." He frowned at her. "Daisy Donovan, you're going to marry me, next weekend as a matter of fact. Enough lollygagging and floating around. I've pursued you for years, and whether you want to admit it or not, you've enjoyed being the princess of my passion."

She raised a brow. "I'm not getting married."

"Yeah, you are." He sipped his tea, stuffing more pumpkin muffin into his mouth. "Eat up. If you're eating for four, you're going to need your strength."

His blood got weird, sort of wobbly, when he voiced aloud the idea that he was going to be a father to triplets. A triple whammy. Still, he'd seen three of his friends adapt quite nicely to the father role, and the good news was, between the four of them, they could now field a decent-sized girls' soccer team. He pondered that. Heck, counting Justin's new one, if it was a girl, they were well on their way to having enough to justify buying their own bus for the Hanging H.

"John, I'm not marrying you," Daisy said softly.

He looked up at her. "Those little girls need me. They need their father. I'm going to be a helluva lacrosse coach, you wait and see. I'm not so much for ballet and hair buns and the girlier stuff, but I'll suck it up and work on it."

"We're having boys," Daisy said, and John's head started swimming again.

"Boys?" He gulped. "Three *boys*?"

She solemnly nodded.

"I thought everyone in Bridesmaids Creek had girls. That's why there's, like, five thousand women to every man here. There's something in the creek water that does it." He slipped off his Stetson, wiped his brow, realized he was still light-headed, and was babbling like a baby. The muffins weren't helping his sudden brain fog.

She'd blown his mind. Again.

"Strangely, we're having boys." Daisy reached for a muffin. "And as I know your family raised you on the circuit, I hope you'll appreciate that I want something more stable for my sons."

He blinked, came back to earth. So that was what this sudden meeting was about. *Her* sons. She was staking out territory, letting him know that she didn't want an itinerant lifestyle for their family—in which she didn't appear to be including him.

Yet in his heart, he believed that she was meant to be his. He didn't know how, he just knew it in his gut.

Plus, he didn't think the wise elderly troublemakers— er, pillars—of Bridesmaids Creek would have revealed one of its major secrets to him unless they considered him a favored son, and even an important part of this town and this woman's life. Cosette, after all, had never given up her matchmaker's crown, even though she'd lost her shop.

No, they'd revealed secrets to him because they didn't want him to give up hope. He was the guardian of the magic.

John dived into the wellspring of hope they'd gifted him. "Daisy, listen. Whatever you want is fine with me." He swallowed, his throat dry, completely aware for the first time that the sexy woman across from him regarded him as an obstacle of sorts, maybe even an enemy.

Oh, hell, who was he kidding? She'd never given him an ounce of encouragement. He didn't even know why she'd made love to him, unless she'd only wanted a child.

She'd been on that funky medication. But she claimed

she hadn't wanted *his* child. Which would really dent his ego massively, except Cosette and Jane claimed she'd been a virgin. Still, how the hell would they know? Daisy was a grown woman, she wasn't going to share her exploits—

He shut down that train of thought. He knew he was her first.

"Daisy, you were a virgin. I know you were."

She eyed him steadily. "So?"

He grinned, the whole matter going crystal clear for him. "So, either you're not being honest because you're trying to get the upper hand here—very Robert Donovan of you—or you're not letting your subconscious tell you the truth." He reached across, took that delicate little hand of hers that had always wrapped around him so sweetly in his. "You were taking medication to get pregnant. You chose to seduce me, little lady. That means either you wanted me or you wanted my baby or both, but it's time for you to start telling both of us the truth."

THE PROBLEM WITH John was that he was annoyingly macho, Daisy thought, feeling his big paw engulf her hand. He had no idea how sexy he was, and by all rights, she shouldn't have fallen for a man who'd lived out of a trailer most of his life. It didn't make sense. But the thing was, she was in love with him, and that love had made her do stupid things.

Like hop in the sack with him every chance she got.

In fact, she'd like to hop in a sack with him right now—her whole body seemed to miss his, miss him—but she was going to fight it with everything she had.

"How far along are you?"

She hesitated. "You should know. Six months."

He grinned, so happy, and so handsome because he was that happy, that she tugged her hand out of his grasp. "Don't look so thrilled."

"I am thrilled. I'm over the moon. Hey, Jane!"

"Don't!" she hissed, but when had John ever listened to anything?

"Daisy and I are having triplets!" he told Jane, his voice carrying to the diners who'd begun pouring in for breakfast once the doors had opened.

Daisy felt her face turn red, her neck burning with embarrassment. "John!"

Jane grinned at Daisy. "Well, what do you know? That medication our resident quack gives out strikes again! Hey, everybody, muffins on the house to celebrate Daisy and John's new triplets!"

A roar went up, and applause, and the diner burst into chatter. She glared at John, who was glancing around at everyone, waving hello to this person and that, and generally enjoying his moment as the big man of Bridesmaids Creek.

"Was that necessary?" Daisy demanded.

"To share our good news with our friends? Indeed it was." He winked at her. "I don't mind public opinion helping me to shanghai you to the altar, beautiful."

She sniffed. "I've never bowed to public pressure."

He laughed. "I'm going to marry you, Daisy Donovan. And you're going to ask me nicely to do so."

She rolled her eyes, but couldn't deny his claim as well-wishers began crowding their booth. She didn't think she'd ever seen John look happier than he was at this moment.

It was endearing, and it was sexy. Daisy felt a bit of

the glow steal over her, finally living one of the big BC moments that had always seemed to escape her.

But it couldn't last. And no one knew that better than her.

Chapter Seven

"Into bed you go." John took her home, placing her tenderly in his bed in the bunkhouse. "A little nap is good for the soul, they say. I'm sure you're jet-lagged, and you really should be resting up for my three sons. They're going to keep you very busy in a few months."

Daisy told her heart this wasn't exactly where it wanted to be, eyeing him as he tucked her into the covers. "I'm not much of a napper."

He looked at her. "You look a bit pale. I'll get you some water. Air travel is dehydrating."

"I don't want to be smothered during this pregnancy." She tried not to notice how manly and lean he looked in his worn jeans. "It'll be a long few more months if you mother-hen me."

"You rest. Then we'll proceed." He tucked a strand of her hair behind her ear, and Daisy basked in the feeling of being revered. It was certainly a novelty for her—but John had always treated her this way, she realized.

Her heart warmed even more.

"Proceed with what?"

"We have a lot of planning to do." He landed next to her in the bed but didn't touch her, practically hung on the edge, creating distance. "I have to close my eyes now. My brain's on overload."

She didn't know if she could rest with him so close to her. Surely he should be trying to kiss her.

Of course he should be trying to kiss her. She *wanted* him to kiss her.

He began to snore instead. Daisy sucked in an outraged breath. In Montana, all she'd had to do was think *bed* and John had seemed to appear to tumble her into one. If not a bed, then a hallway, a blanket near a wooded stream—even once on a cliff top gazing up at the stars. Parts of her that shouldn't get warm not only warmed but wished for John—who was resting his "overloaded" brain with enthusiasm, judging from the expulsion of jetlike snores coming from his handsome frame—to wake up and focus on the way they'd created these children she was now carrying.

Daisy reached over, gave him a tap.

"Mmm?" he asked, the snores coming to a full stop.

"The doctor says it won't be much longer before I lose my, er, sexy—"

"I'm on it. No worries." He patted her hand, rolled onto his side facing the wall.

Okay, that hadn't worked.

"Also, I'll be on bed rest, probably in a few weeks."

"Sounds good to me. We can start now, if you like."

She didn't reply, and soft snores began to emit from him again. "John Lopez Mathison, I think you're playing hard to get."

"I am. It's working, too." He rolled over, scooped her against him, kissing the back of her neck, shooting tingles all over her. "If you sleep off some jet leg, I promise to buy you an ice-cream cone at the Haunted

H tonight. You'll be surprised how much that place has changed now that you got it moved to the creek."

His arm tucked solidly around her, holding her to him in the most intimate way. He was being dense, as dense as a thick, night-shrouded forest, but this felt good, too—and he *had* received a shock. Rest was probably a restorative for his bachelor system—so Daisy relaxed into his warmth and fell asleep.

"SORRY," JOHN SAID, waking he wasn't sure how much later. But clearly he'd napped for hours, as the sun was beaming high outside. "I didn't mean to pass out on you." He had a delicious brunette in his arms, his dream come true—and he'd sacked out like a large bag of potatoes.

"I'm sure the news was hard for you."

He released Daisy and sat up, trying to remember what chores he was on the list for this afternoon that he might be late for. "No, I'm happy about the babies. I appreciate you coming home to tell me in person. The old ladies dragged me out of bed last night and I missed about six of my eight typical, desired sleep hours."

"The old ladies?"

John tugged on his boots. "Cosette and Jane. That was probably disrespectful. I should have said, the time-enhanced matchmakers of BC."

Daisy giggled. "They kidnapped you?"

"They encouraged me to join them for some late-night high jinks." He leaned over and dropped a fast kiss on her lips. "That's to keep you happy until later."

"Later when you plan to ravish me?"

He laughed. "Later when I get you that ice-cream cone I promised you. Make yourself at home, if you want. I've got to get to my chores. I'll be done in about eight hours."

She swung her legs over the side of the bed, and John thought he'd never seen a more sexy woman. "I still need to see Dad."

He felt a tremor of unease. "Okay, so I'll get you for dinner, then take you down to the new and improved Haunted H."

"Sounds good." She smiled at him. "Remember what I told you."

"Remember what I told *you*."

She raised a brow. "That you're going to get me a cone tonight?"

"That I'm going to marry you, and you're going to ask me nicely to do it." He grinned. "And if your doctor's right and you're going to be couch-bound very soon, you'd better hurry, beautiful, if you want some of what you were trying to get from me a little while ago."

"You think highly of yourself, don't you?"

"I think highly of you."

"Here's the thing, John," Daisy said, taking a deep breath, and he heard it—the I-can't-marry-you-because— so he cut her off as fast as he could. Whatever it was, they'd deal with it. If it was Robert, they'd deal with him and so on. Nothing was going to keep him from Daisy and his sons—not anymore.

"I've got to run," he interrupted, before she could get to the juicy part that was sure to make him cry. "You save that thought for later."

"All right."

She actually looked a little relieved. John dropped his hat on his head, decided against stealing one more fast kiss, and headed out the door. She followed, hopping onto her motorcycle.

He frowned. "Daisy, I'd like you to give up the bike while you're pregnant."

She shrugged. "I'd like you to give up letting Cosette and Jane drag you around in the middle of the night."

"Why?"

"Because they'll eventually get you into trouble. They're very sweet and very darling, and I love them dearly, but I feel like anything that's done in the dark in BC might be dangerous."

He grinned. "You just remember that tonight when you tap on my back again. Interrupting a man's REMs for a little sexy playtime. Whatever were you thinking?" Now he did kiss her—he could no longer resist it—especially as she'd let out a demure little gasp at his comment, her lips parting too prettily to pass up. She clung to him, surprising him a little.

"Tonight I'm all yours," he told her.

"I flew two days to be with you. Be ready to do more than talk."

John laughed, tipped his hat and headed for the barn, thinking there had never been a saucier, sassier lady. And the way things were going, she was soon going to be all his. Mrs. Daisy Mathison.

It had a very nice ring to it.

Which reminded him, he needed a ring to do an honorable proposal—when she finally got up the courage to ask him. And he *was* going to make her ask him—she'd waited far too long to cast her dark eyes his way.

Daisy Donovan was going to have to jump off the spot and fight for *him* for a change. He whistled, everything in his life looking up, skyward, even. He was going to be a father, he was about to have a wife.

That BC charm stuff *really* had some kick to it.

"I CAN'T FIX this for you." Robert Donovan gazed at his only daughter, his eyes sorrowful. "I wish I could. I'd spend all my fortune to see you happy, Daisy."

"I know." Daisy sat in the garden room with her father, gazing pensively at the beautiful statues and blooming flowers outside.

"When are you going to tell him?"

"Soon. Tonight." Daisy took a deep breath. "I tried to today, but he cut me off. Almost like he knew I was going to drop some bad news on him."

"He's no dummy." Robert leaned back in his favorite chair and sighed. "I actually have a lot of respect for John Mathison, as I told you when I called you in Australia to tell you of his visit. He was a little opinionated, but that didn't trouble me. I rather appreciated him stating his case for my little girl with such enthusiasm."

Daisy managed a smile, but the man who walked into the room next made her hesitate. "Ty, what are you doing here?"

"I invited him," Robert said. "Welcome home, son."

He got up to hug the son he'd discovered two years ago. Daisy didn't know what to do, so she remained seated. As much work as she had to do to make it up to people in Bridesmaids Creek, she wasn't sure what to do with a new half brother. Ty Spurlock was a good man and a SEAL, obviously on leave from the Navy, home to see Jade and their new twins.

"Daisy," Ty said, nodding in her direction, and Daisy nodded back, feeling very out of her element now that she and her half brother had been called home at the same time so the father they shared could speak to them. "Congratulations on the triplets." He grinned, completely comfortable, a happily married man and favored town son.

"This is all your fault," Daisy said. "You brought a bunch of bachelors to town to find brides."

"And you fell right into the trap?" Ty laughed and took the seat Robert gestured him to. "Don't feel bad. I fell into my own trap before you did."

"Speaking of traps," Robert said, "Daisy doesn't want to get married."

Ty grinned at her. "She will when the time is right."

Daisy was shocked by this show of support. She looked at her father to see how he was taking Ty's comment. As she suspected, her father looked none too pleased.

"I asked you here today for a couple of reasons, one of which was to help me convince your sister that she has to marry this John." He mused silently for a moment. "Believe me, that's not an easy thing for me to say. I never thought I'd be talking about marrying my little girl to a man formerly named Squint." He brightened. "However, he has convinced me that he has my daughter's best interests at heart, and that he loves you, Daisy. Trust me, you don't want to pass up love."

"You can pass it up," Ty said. "If you don't love my buddy, just tell him you don't love him. He'll be devastated, he'll follow you around like a puppy for the rest of your life because you're having his children, and you'll always have all the support and backup you ever needed because he's that kind of guy. He'll never ask you a second time, because he's got too much pride, so it'll never be awkward or weird for you."

"It's already awkward," Daisy said. "I'm pregnant with triplets. And we were as careful as could be."

"Then it was meant to be." Ty seemed quite amused by this. "You got hit by the BC magic. Isn't that what you always wanted?"

"Tell your brother why you don't want to marry the father of your children," Robert urged.

"When I met his family, I met his two brothers. Who, by the way, are very nice. But Javier happened to mention that John has never been in a relationship for very long. They never *stuck*, was the word he used."

"So?" Ty shrugged. "Most of us hadn't. It's no reason not to give the man a chance."

"But that's the thing," Daisy said. "I've never been in a relationship at all!"

Her father and brother stared at her.

"Oh," Ty said, "I forgot about that. I guess I always assumed with that gaggle of boys hanging around you that one of them—"

"No," Daisy said. "I never dated any of my friends."

"They were in love with you," Robert said.

"So they claim." She sighed. "And that's how I'm going to renew Bridesmaids Creek. It's going to be my ultimate act to ingratiate myself into a town I want desperately to accept me."

"How?" Ty asked.

"Get married," Robert said. "If you throw a wedding party, you'll be forgiven. Around here, forgiveness comes with a couple slices of wedding cake real easily. Haven't you noticed?"

Daisy frowned at her father. "Dad, I don't think John

and I have what it takes to be parents together. According to his brother, John's never stayed in the same place more than a few years, as a consequence of the way they were raised. Not that Javier and Jackson were complaining. They just noted that their way of life isn't for everyone."

"Let me get this straight." Ty leaned back in his chair, smiling his thanks when the butler put a tray on the table in front of them. It had a whiskey decanter, some glasses, some soda and small edibles. "You guys live differently here, don't you?"

"Thank you, Barclay," Daisy said to the butler as he mixed them up some whiskey and sodas. "Just some sparkling water for me, please."

"Anyway," Ty continued, "if I understand you correctly, you're afraid."

"Not exactly," Daisy shot back.

"You don't want to raise your children on the road. In a trailer, going from rodeo to rodeo."

"We're having boys," Daisy said. "Eventually John's going to remember how he grew up."

"Maybe he didn't like it," Robert said.

"I'm going to ask him," Ty said thoughtfully. "I'll just say, 'Hey, John, old buddy, are you planning on raising your boys in rodeo?'"

"Would you mind?" Daisy asked. "I don't want to ask him."

"Why? The man isn't quiet about his opinions," Robert said. "He'd tell you."

"It's a hard life. And he has restless feet."

"Says the woman who ran off to Montana after another man." Ty grinned at her, holding up a hand when she began to protest. "I know, I know, that's when you fell for my pal. But you can't put all this on him."

Daisy shook her head. "Eventually he'd regret marrying me."

"Why? Because you're such a good person?" Ty looked at her curiously. "Because you're going to be an awesome mother?"

Daisy felt tears well in her eyes. "I don't know how."

The men stared at her.

"Ah," Ty said slowly. "Now we're getting down to the truth. You don't feel like you deserve John Mathison. You think you're going to let him down. You're afraid you're not going to be a good mother."

Robert looked misty. "That's not going to happen. You're going to be a wonderful mother."

"Why? How?" She wiped at her nose. "I haven't been a particularly good anything in my life."

They sat quietly, sipping their whiskeys. Daisy put a hand on her stomach as she looked out into the beautiful garden. Occasionally she could feel the babies move inside her. In time, they'd get even more active.

Very soon she'd be bed bound.

"Daisy, listen."

She glanced up at Ty, waiting.

"We'll all be here for you. If you don't want to marry the man, you don't have to," he said softly. He reached out, touched her hand. "We've given you a bit of rough road over the years, sure. But the thing is, we're going to take care of you, because that's what Bridesmaids Creek does. We take care of each other."

Daisy felt giant tears leap to her eyes and threaten to slide down her cheeks. "Thank you," she murmured.

"There now," Robert said. "It'll all work out eventually. It always does."

Daisy shook her head, the words sounding a trifle incongruous from the man who had once been the most hated in the town. She felt a huge burden from that, too. Her parents—and Ty's—hadn't even had a happy marriage. How would she know how to make a happy marriage? And it wasn't totally the way Ty said it was; they had given her a lot of rough road, but she'd deserved a lot of it, too.

She'd feel better when she'd had time to make amends.

She'd feel better when she had a better sense of who she was.

Barclay reentered the room, and Daisy thought he was coming to refresh the tray. But then she realized there was a man joining their family gathering, and to her astonishment, she saw that it was John.

What was even more astonishing was the giant leap her heart made inside her, as if it recognized the man of her dreams, and the only man for her.

Chapter Eight

"Sit down, sit down," Robert said genially, pointing to a seat near him. He eyed Daisy's gang who had followed John into the room. "Barclay, if we could have some more whiskeys and snacks, please."

They all seated themselves, her gang gazing at John like slightly uncomfortable combatants. He seemed immune to their displeasure.

"It's good to see you, man." John reached over and slapped Ty on the back. "When did you return to BC?"

"This morning. Went to see my wife and little girls, then came straight here. Have yet to pay a call to the Hanging H, but I hear you've been keeping everything in good shape."

"Not to cut the happy reunion short, fellows," Daisy said, "but I'm glad you're all here. I have something to say."

Her father and their guests turned to her in surprise.

"Wedding plans?" John said.

"No." Daisy shook her head.

"Ah. I thought maybe these gentlemen were going to offer to be my ushers or something." John gave them a grin that said he was more than aware of their disapprobation with him, and really didn't care.

"John, we're not discussing anything relating to a wedding," Daisy said.

John smiled at Daisy, and her heart jumped. The gleam in his eyes told her that he wasn't about to give up on the idea of marrying her. In spite of everything she'd told her father and brother, didn't she want to marry him?

I'm just so scared. Marriage wasn't a good thing for my father and mother. I've heard the stories, and they weren't the stuff of dreams and fairy tales.

"Anyway," Daisy said, "I have a lot to do in a small amount of time, so I have to be really organized. I hope you won't mind me springing this on you all at once, but I'm hoping that you'll consider giving up your lease so that Cosette and Phillipe can have that space again for their shops. Madame and Monsieur Matchmaker need to be back where they belong. They're an important part of the magic of BC."

Dig, Clint, Gabriel, Red and Carson stared at her, as did John and her father. "I'll help you find another place for your dating service and business."

"We were just about to think about franchising," Red said, unhappy.

"Franchising?" Daisy stared at her "gang," stunned. "Are you even profitable yet?"

"You'd be surprised. Cigar sales are booming," Gabriel said.

"I thought your core business is a dating service," John said.

"It is," Clint said. "But we're finding that cigars are where it's at. Especially high-end cigars."

Daisy and John glanced at each other. He shrugged,

clearly not sure what to make of the new "business" in town. Daisy looked at her father, who also shrugged.

"Would you consider moving your cigar bar?" Daisy asked. "So that we can get some equilibrium back in BC?"

Red shook his head. "That's a primo location. Easy for out-of-towners to find."

Daisy considered that. "So your customers are mostly from surrounding towns?"

"Yes, that's right," Dig said. "But honestly, we've got a whopping mail-order business, too. And sometimes folks come in from the big city."

Daisy shook her head. "I had no idea."

"You haven't been here," Gabriel said gently. "You've been in Montana and other places."

"And when you *are* here, your attention is divided." Clint slid a glance at John. "You haven't been hanging with us like you used to, Daze."

She sighed. "This is all my fault. I got Phillipe and Cosette out of their comfortable space, because I was being selfish. But I didn't understand what I was taking from them, what I was taking from BC."

She was really, really sad about that. And now there was no way to fix it, which was not good for the older couple. Their marriage had suffered because of the financial distress she'd helped cause.

"But you've done a lot of good, too," Carson pointed out. "You've changed so much, Daze, we hardly recognize you anymore."

The lights flickered. Daisy glanced out toward the garden, realizing it had gotten very dark outside. The sky was steel gray. She looked at John, and he smiled at her. She felt instantly better.

"I agree with your friends. You've done good things lately, Daisy." John glanced at Robert. "And you're not the only one who's turned into a productive and upstanding citizen."

Robert raised his glass to the gathering. Ty and everyone raised their glasses back.

"Here's to remaking BC," Robert said. "I would like to say that Daisy's idea of moving the Haunted H to the creek was brilliant."

"Remember when the Haunted H was a liability?" Ty grinned at Robert. "We were convinced you were deliberately trying to kill people out there to run off business."

The lights flickered again and Daisy looked to the window. "I'd better make this quick so you guys can hit the road."

"Take your time." Carson held up his glass. "We've got no place better to be than right here with our nearest and dearest."

She said with a little apprehension, "Those days of taking over businesses aren't over, Carson."

"What do you mean?" Her gang gazed at her from their comfortable chairs, lulled into complacency by her father's good whiskey. Carson shot her a quizzical look.

"I'd like to buy out your dating service." She looked at all of them in turn.

"But we haven't gotten it off the ground yet," Dig said. "We've been so busy with the cigar bar."

Daisy went to sit by John. "Name your price. We're in the market for a dating business."

John caught her hand in his. "I like it when you wheel and deal. But not so much that you don't get enough rest for my boys."

Every eye in the room bounced to her stomach and then over to John.

"Heck, we'd let you have it for free, Daisy," Gabriel said. His friends nodded. "Friends don't charge friends. We'll incorporate you into our business."

"I'll take you up on that." Daisy glanced at John. "You're now the proud owner of a dating service."

"Which will become Madame Matchmaker's Premier Matchmaking Services once again?" He grinned at her.

"We'll see how it works out." The lights flickered again, and then went out altogether. Five lighter flames instantly sparked to life in the room.

Daisy looked at her gang, their faces glowing in the dim light. "Really? I feel like I'm at a concert."

"Can't have a cigar business without fire. Where's your candles, Robert?" Red asked.

"There are some decorative ones on the table there you can use," her father replied. "The generator will be on in a moment. And Barclay will no doubt be in with news."

John's phone buzzed. Daisy turned to him as he pulled it out, scanned it.

"The sheriff says a tornado has touched down in town," he said, reading further. "He wants everyone to stay inside in safe locations." He looked at Daisy. "There's no warning siren out here, I take it?"

"None this far out. In fact, there's really not anything like that in town, is there, Dad?"

He shook his head. "Not to my knowledge. Even if there was, it wouldn't reach us or the Hanging H. We should probably have one put in."

"Hang on," John said, looking at his phone again.

"Dennis says…" He stopped. She saw his face tighten with concern. "There was a direct hit on the creek. The Haunted H is gone."

Daisy gasped. The whole room went still. It was a strange tableau with everyone staring at each other by lighter and candlelight. Barclay strolled in with a huge flashlight to set on the table. It threw a wide beam on the ceiling, relieving the darkness.

"The generator will come on any minute," Barclay told Robert. "The foreman and the groundskeeper are checking it over now."

"Thank you." Barclay left and Robert looked at John. "My phone isn't working. Do you still have cell service?"

"It's weak, but I have it," John said. "Of course, out here in the county cell service can be spotty at the best of times."

"My phone's working." Daisy turned to John. "Dennis's text says nobody was hurt. But I feel like we ought to go see what we can do to help out at the Haunted H."

"No," her father said. "My advice is you stay right here."

"Your father's right." The lights came on, and John stood. "The sheriff said he wanted everyone to stay put, in case of another tornado. To relieve your mind, I'll drive to the creek and see what needs to be done immediately."

"I'll ride shotgun," Ty said, rising.

"Bring anyone here who needs shelter," Daisy said, and Robert nodded.

"Absolutely. It's safer here than anywhere in town," he said. "We have plenty of room."

Barclay came in with another tray of food and drinks.

Daisy looked at him. "Barclay, would you mind packing up some food and first-aid items for John to take to town with him?"

"I'm coming with you." Daisy rose, and every man in the room said, "No!"

"All right!" She sank back down. "It's going to be a long pregnancy for all of us."

Her gang rose. "We'll follow him. We'll keep a close eye on John, and make sure he gets back to you in one piece."

"Watch out," she told John. "Once they appoint themselves your good friends and protectors, you'll always have your own squad looking out for you."

John looked at the five men doubtfully. "I'm used to traveling alone."

"Not anymore, you're not. If I can't go, you can't go alone," Daisy said.

"Fair's fair, I guess." He looked at Robert. "I don't have to ask if you'll make sure she rests."

"We have it under control." Robert waved them on. "Let us know what we can do to help."

As soon as the seven men left, Daisy turned to her father. "Are you sure this isn't going to be too much for you?"

"I'm not doing anything, except maybe giving a few people shelter."

"I just don't want you taking on too much. One of the reasons I came back was that I was worried about you. You're still not exercising." She gazed at her father. "It wasn't that long ago that you gave us all a scare."

He hmmphed. "I'm fine. Barclay makes sure I get all kinds of vegetables. Very little red meat, no cakes or treats after every meal. Special occasions only. It's giving him the chance to boss me around, which he enjoys."

Daisy stood. "I'm going to call Cosette and Jane. Make sure they're all right."

"Those two will outlive us all."

Daisy laughed. "Probably. I'll be right back."

She went up to her room for some privacy. "Cosette? It's Daisy. Are you all right?"

"I'm fine. Phillipe's fine." Cosette sighed. "Did you hear? The Haunted H is gone!"

"I heard. It's terrible. But as long as no one was hurt, it can be rebuilt." She looked out the window at the dark skies, still too gray and bruised-looking for her comfort. The faster John came home, the better she'd feel.

Home? When did you start thinking of this as his home?

It wasn't. John would be more comfortable on the road than here. This would never be home for the father of her children.

She would never be home on the road. She wasn't like Mrs. Mathison, who could raise three boys in a trailer, following the rodeo circuit.

I'm having three boys. He's going to want them to be rodeo people. Why wouldn't he? It's what he knows. And there's nothing wrong with that at all.

"Are you there, Daisy?" Cosette asked. "I asked how you're feeling."

"Oh. I feel fine." Daisy sank onto her bed. "I'm just worried about Mackenzie and Suz and you guys. I feel terrible about the Haunted H. It was my idea to move it to Bridesmaids Creek." And now it was gone.

"Daisy, you couldn't have known. You were trying

to help. Frankly, the creek was a very successful location for the Haunted H. Visitors really liked it being in a wooded area, too. Especially a place where we have often held our charmed swims."

"I'm in shock that it's gone." She felt almost adrift by how her idea had affected Suz and Mackenzie's business, and the town itself, now leveled, almost extinguished.

"Every town has to grow or it dies. Daisy, don't blame this on yourself. You didn't cause the tornado." Cosette was silent for a moment. "Did you hear that mine and Phillipe's old shops, and the jail, are gone, too?"

"Gone?" Daisy was horrified.

"Every last stick and twig." Cosette sighed. "Check your phone when we get off. I'm sure you got the text, too."

Tears jumped into Daisy's eyes. "We'll rebuild Bridesmaids Creek, Cosette. We'll put our town back together."

"I know." Cosette sniffed. "We have a lot to be grateful for. No one got hurt. As far as I know, not even a cow was injured."

"Okay. That's the best news of all. I've got to get back to Dad. I'll check on you and Jane and Mackenzie and everybody in a little bit."

"Be sure to rest. The best thing to do is keep yourself healthy. We'll all get through this. Together."

They hung up and Daisy went back to her father.

"The jail is gone, and the fellows aren't going to be too happy to learn that their new cigar bar has been lost." Daisy sat near her father. "All these years nothing so much as a tornado sighting, and then suddenly the town takes a direct hit." She burst into tears, finally overcome by what she'd been trying so hard to hold back. "If I hadn't insisted that Suz and Mackenzie move their business to the creek, it would still be operating. I'm too embarrassed to call." She took a deep breath, wiped her eyes. "Of course I will, just as soon as I have a grip on myself."

Robert shook his head. "You can't blame this on yourself. And no one else will, either, Daisy."

"I wish I hadn't always been such a negative spirit in BC."

He sighed heavily. "They say the sins of the fathers visit on the children. To be honest, I started us off on the wrong foot here. I didn't take care of your mother, and I've always regretted that. I wanted to be king of all I surveyed, but in the end, it never made me as happy as my family does. It's a lesson that came late, I'm afraid, and that it's affected you, too."

"I don't know, Dad." She reached over to touch his hand. "We can do our best going forward to build the town up, and help people."

"It's really all we can do. But it's a plan I like."

They sat looking out at the garden, the dark skies seeming to bring night on even faster than usual. "The sheriff isn't going to know what to do without his jail."

Robert laughed softly. "We'll start there. We have to have law and order in Bridesmaids Creek."

For some reason, that made both of them smile. Daisy didn't know if there'd ever been anyone in the lonely jail cells. But it was Dennis's place, and it stood as a solid center of BC. "Okay. We'll have to help with the Haunted H, and the center of town."

He nodded. "I think I'll sell a few buildings I've got in other countries."

She looked at her father. "Why?"

"I don't need the biggest kingdom. What I need is right here in BC." He reached out, took her hand in his. "I've got you, and Ty and my grandchildren. That's really all the kingdom I want these days."

She smiled. "So you're planning to really step up for Bridesmaids Creek?"

"If there's something we can do to help, it wouldn't do any good to leave cash sitting around in our bank accounts."

"No, it wouldn't." Daisy grinned. "And I'm sitting on a little plan of my own concerning BC. I'm taking over the dating service, and I'm going to take lessons from our resident matchmaker."

Robert whistled. "That'll be an education of a different stripe."

"Exactly." She nodded. "And I have my first victims in my sights."

Chapter Nine

Daisy looked at the text when it came in two hours later. Done what we can do here, for now.

She hesitated, then replied, Are you coming back here?

Her breath was trapped in her lungs as she waited. It was the first time she'd ever invited John to her home, and surely he'd get that he was being invited to spend the night.

If that's what you want.

I want, she wrote back.

I'm on the front porch.

She shot out of bed and hurried down the stairs, pulling open the front door. John was, in fact, standing right there, grinning.

"Thanks for coming back."

"My family's here. My lady, and my three sons. Where else would I go?"

"No place." She smiled and pulled him inside and up the stairs to her room.

"What about your father? Barclay? The pillars of Bridesmaids Creek?" John asked.

She kissed him. "My father is a few thousand feet away, and would be worried if you weren't here. Nobody in town needed to come back here for shelter?"

"No. The damage is extensive, but most everybody was at home when the worst hit."

She was delighted when he kissed her, too, drawing her to him. "I was glad you were safe in this fortress," John said. "But I missed you."

"I missed you, too." He kissed her fingertips, making Daisy shiver.

"Is it really horrible?"

"We'll be rebuilding for a while."

They sank onto the bed, and he put a hand on her stomach. "But I don't want you worrying. I don't want you starting a committee to fund-raise or do anything like that. Resting is all I want you to do."

"Too late," she said. "You knew better than that."

"Yeah, I just wanted to see how much I could get away with."

"Not much." She kissed him again. "Thanks for coming back. I was afraid you wouldn't."

He raised a brow. "It's going to be hard for you to get rid of me now that you're having my children."

"Is that the only reason?"

John kissed her gently, lingering over her lips. "Yes."

Daisy laughed. "That's mean."

"It's important to keep you guessing."

"I suppose that's fair."

He kissed her belly. "I knew you'd figure out that I was the best catch around eventually. I just waited for you to come to your senses."

She was so glad he was back—and safe—that she didn't want to pepper him with questions. "Do you want to shower? I'll go get you some coffee and food. You have to be starving."

"That sounds great." He suddenly sounded tired as he tossed his belt onto a nearby chair. "Are you sure Robert's going to be okay with me being here?"

"Haven't you noticed a distinct thawing in his manner lately?" Daisy glanced at him as she hung in the doorway.

"Yeah, what's that all about?"

She smiled. "We'll discuss that later. You shower. But yes, Dad will be glad you're here. And glad for anyone else that needs a place to stay."

Daisy went downstairs, dialed the Hanging H. Suz answered. "Suz, it's Daisy."

"Hi," Suz said, and she sounded sad.

"Listen, Suz, I should come by to tell you this, but John isn't keen on me being out at the moment."

"And he's right! You don't go anywhere! There's downed trees everywhere and all kinds of debris scattered around."

"I know." Daisy swallowed. "Suz, I'm sorry, more sorry than I can say, about the Haunted H. I wish I'd never suggested you move it there."

"Daisy, you didn't plan the path of the tornado. You couldn't have known. We'll rebuild bigger and better than ever and be ready for another Bridesmaids Creek swim or Best Man's Fork race."

But when would that be? "We should do that soon."

"We need a new influx of bachelors for that to happen," Suz reminded her. "We have no shortage of bride-worthy material."

"It'll be a long time before BC gets cleaned up enough to handle large crowds."

"Well," Suz said on a deep sigh, "we've rebuilt before. Sometimes it feels like it's a snakebit project, but then I see all the happy kids coming with their families, and I realize the Haunted H was a dream my parents had that needs to stay alive."

"I agree. Good night, Suz," Daisy said.

"You listen to John," Suz said. "Those babies of yours need all the rest they can get, because when they come out, you're going to be busy! You're having one more than I did, and trust me, life is crazy these days!"

Daisy hung up, gathered some hot coffee, tea, a small bit of whiskey in case John wanted it, and warmed up some pot roast and veggies from dinner. Barclay came in, took a glance at her tray and added a cloth napkin, some fresh cookies and utensils.

"Thank you, Barclay."

"I'll carry it. Up you go, Miss Daisy."

"I can—"

"In another few months you can," he said, very respectfully, and that was that. Daisy followed him up the stairs and to her room, amazed that John was already out of the shower, with a towel slung on his waist, barking orders on his cell phone.

"There's hot cocoa in the pot for you, Miss Daisy," Barclay said, and filtered out.

John hung up and looked at the assortment of food. "Thanks. I'm starved."

She nodded. "I know. I figured you would be—" she began, realizing his eyes were locked on her. Heat shot through her, and she managed a slight smile. "You have to eat first," she said softly. "Barclay will get his feelings hurt."

John went to the tray, fixed himself a whiskey, watching her as she made a space at a small table near her window for him to sit.

"I like this side of you."

"Domestic?"

"Caring."

"I suppose I haven't given you that much opportunity to see that I do have a soft side." She sat in the flowered, skirted chair across from him. "I just talked to Suz."

"I know. Cisco called me, playing the part of the concerned husband." He dug into the pot roast and vegetables with obvious pleasure.

"Concerned about what?"

"Oh, I think they don't want anyone to know that the Hanging H sustained a little bit of a wind shear at the ranch."

"What?" Daisy's heart skipped a beat. "Is there a lot of damage?"

"A little bit of damage to their roof, apparently. They don't want to make a fuss about it, though, because they're afraid people will rush over there to help them. There's a lot of folks in town who need help, and they want all resources going to the people who really need it."

"What are they going to do?"

"Right now, they've got some guys on the roof covering it with a tarp. This is great food."

"Thanks," she murmured. "What about Suz and the babies?"

"Well, remember Suz and Cisco live in a house they built on the property. I think Cisco's more worried about

Mackenzie and her crowd of four, and since she's pregnant again—"

"She needs to come here," Daisy said quickly. "With the babies. They can't be there with all that banging going on. The children will never be able to rest."

"Are you sure you have enough space?"

She looked at him. "There's a spare bedroom or two," she said, not wanting to share that there were ten rooms that could be used for bedrooms alone.

"Robert wouldn't mind? Barclay won't give notice if four little girls start running around his perfectly kept domain?"

She slowly shook her head. "Barclay would love to have more people here to take care of. Years ago, Dad hired him away from several families who shared his services. Barclay is used to busy, and around here, it's just Dad, and sometimes me."

He dragged her onto the bed with him. She wanted desperately to pull off his towel, hang on to him, make love to him. But sadness hung over both of them, and she could tell he was tired, and that he was holding back everything he'd done at the creek. No doubt he'd hauled, towed and helped the sheriff digest the loss of his jail, too. It was a devastating blow to everyone. She sensed his mood, felt the tension and tiredness in his muscles.

So the towel stayed, but she remained in his arms, held tightly, securely. And there was no place she would rather be.

SOMETHING WOKE DAISY, and she lay in bed for a few seconds, disoriented, wondering if she'd merely heard a branch tapping on a windowpane. Then she realized what had awakened her was that John wasn't in bed with her. The place beside her was cool, as if he'd been gone awhile.

She hopped out of bed, dressed and went looking for him.

"Barclay, did John say where he was going?" She went into the kitchen, took the hot tea the butler offered her but didn't sit. She wouldn't be here long.

"I believe Mr. Mathison mentioned he was needed in town, Miss Daisy."

Barclay usually didn't hold back details from her, and she sensed he was now. "Why are you up at this hour, Barclay?"

He fixed a tray of fresh vegetables with a side of yummy-looking hummus. "Mr. Mathison asked me to prepare you a nutritious meal, organic, when you awakened."

"Yes, but I'm not usually up at three in the morning, and neither are you." She looked narrowly at him. "So, why are you pretending that you're awake to give me carrots and dip?"

Barclay shook his head. "It's not my place to note the comings and goings of our guests, Miss Daisy."

This was a new side of Barclay. "Okay. Thank you. Could you put this nutritious snack in a bag for me? I'm going into town." And when she found John, she was going to explain to him that he didn't need to oversee her diet.

What she needed was for him to make love to her.

He hadn't been lukewarm about doing so in Montana.

"Mr. Mathison said he would prefer if you didn't go out, Miss Daisy. He says the roads are dangerous because of fallen tree limbs."

"I'm going out."

"Have the security detail drive you."

She shook her head. "I'll be fine. I promise to stay away from tree limbs." Rain was falling gently outside, but there'd been no notification of more storms on the radio. The power had been restored, at least to their house. She wondered about people farther out in the county than her house.

"Miss Daisy, I fear your father and Mr. Mathison will be very angry with me—"

She grabbed a flashlight. "I'll tell them I sneaked out. Go to bed, Barclay. You deserve the rest."

He followed her to the door. "I haven't rested since you were a little girl, Miss Daisy. Many a night I've stayed up waiting on you."

She smiled at him. "I know," she said softly. "I'll be back soon." Wherever John had gone, she wanted to be with him. She was part of BC, and she wanted to be there for whomever it was that needed help. He wouldn't have left if someone hadn't called for backup. Getting into her truck, she dialed his phone.

No answer. Which was weird, because he always picked up immediately when she called.

She could drive toward town and see if he'd gone to the main area of damage. Maybe cell service still wasn't available there. Light rain began falling again, splattering on the windshield. Daisy made sure her lights were on low and started into town.

To her surprise, she saw John's truck turning onto the main road leading to the creek. Possibly downed trees had damaged something, and he and the sheriff had decided the situation required immediate attention.

"Plus I have the snacks Barclay packed, and the lady

with the snacks is always welcome," she said under her breath, following close behind his truck.

He parked and got out in an area with which she wasn't entirely familiar. She parked beside him, not surprised annoyance was clear on his face when he came to her window. She rolled it down.

"Daisy, go home."

She shook her head. "I want to be part of whatever is going on."

"No." He looked completely put out with her. "Daisy, there is no reason for you to be here, and it's not safe. It's raining, for heaven's sake, and you're pregnant. With triplets."

She'd just so wanted to be with him! "I'll sit in the truck. I promise. I'd feel better if I was here in case—" She glanced around, deciding not to say *in case something happens to you.* "Where's the sheriff?"

"Why would Dennis be here? It's the early hours of the morning."

She looked at him, surprised. "Then why are you here?"

"I can't tell you."

She drew back, annoyed now herself. "You want me to marry you, but you can't tell me what you're doing?"

"It's not that simple." His hair was getting damp, and his shirt was starting to stick to his broad chest and big shoulders, yet he still looked incredibly hot to her. Daisy wondered why it had taken her so darn long to realize just how sexy this man was.

She wished he'd get in the truck and kiss her senseless, maybe even make love to her the way he had in Montana. But something was wrong.

"It is that simple. You got out of my bed and skulked off to the creek without telling me."

He sighed. "I'm sorry. But please go home, babe."

"I'd really like to stay. Especially if the sheriff isn't here to help you with whatever you're going to do." She frowned. "What are you going to do?"

"I'm just making sure everything's safe."

She shivered. "Come back home and get in bed with me."

He smiled. "I'll take you up on that offer. You go warm the bed, and I'll be right there."

"I don't mind waiting."

A tree branch cracked loudly overhead, a sharp sound that made her jump.

"Nothing's safe here." John gave her the sternest look she'd ever seen him wear. "Go home."

She stared at this dark and dangerous man who was suddenly giving her orders. Daisy didn't recall anyone in her life ever giving her an order, and certainly not in that tone. She looked at him, worried.

"I'll be home soon."

"Fine."

"Thank you," he said, his tone softening. "I just want you and the babies to be safe." He made sure her seat belt was secure. "You know I'm crazy about you."

Did she? Of course she did. "I've been spoiled all my life."

He laughed. "I know. It's something I love about you."

"You do?"

"Of course I do. Would I want to marry such a princess if I didn't think I could handle it?"

She frowned. "I'm not a princess."

He laughed again, kissed her through the open window. "Okay."

She turned on the engine. "I don't remember you being so domineering in Montana."

"I wasn't. I didn't have to be. You weren't wandering around in an area where a tornado has recently hit."

"I'll warm up some cocoa for you."

"I'll be there soon."

She pulled away, not liking this at all. Didn't like leaving him here without the sheriff, didn't feel good about him roaming around where tree branches had been weakened by the storm. Rain came down harder even now.

She drove home slowly, carefully minding the roads. Going inside, she put her wrap away and went into the kitchen. Barclay sat there with her father, and a tray of gingerbread.

"It wasn't Barclay's fault," Daisy said with a sigh, and her father nodded.

"I know. Believe me, I know you quite well."

Barclay cut her a slice of gingerbread, warmed it, smoothed a small bit of creamy butter on the top. Daisy breathed in the scent thankfully.

"I've been craving gingerbread, Barclay. Thank you."

"You always liked it when you were a little girl." He poured them all some hot tea.

"So where was your fiancé headed?" her father asked.

"My fiancé?" Daisy thought about that as she took a bite of gingerbread. "I don't think we ever established that."

Robert waved a hand. "He established it when he came over here and gave me what-for about marrying you."

"Did he? Give you what-for?"

Robert raised a brow. "He didn't sound like he much

cared what my opinion on the matter was, and that it was a foregone conclusion. As far as I'm concerned, we'll probably hear wedding bells before those babies are born."

Daisy put a hand over her stomach, feeling the babies shift and move inside. Sometimes it felt like they had an elaborate dance routine going on in there that only they understood. Every time she felt them move, she caught her breath with the wonder of it all.

Sometimes she couldn't believe she was actually having triplets. For a girl who'd always wished her dreams would come true, this time they had. "Anyway, I don't know where John was going. He was being very mysterious. But he'd gone to the creek, and I guess he was going to check on what's left of the Haunted H."

"Not much but twigs, I heard." Robert scowled into his teacup. "Damn shame. But we'll make it bigger next time."

"You old softy." Daisy grinned at her father, then jumped as the doorbell rang. "Who would be here at this hour?"

Barclay went to the door at a pace less formal than usual. Somewhere there had to be an unwritten code that the well-trained butler never hurried.

But Barclay just had. Daisy and her father waited.

Sheriff Dennis made his way into the kitchen, shaking his head at Barclay who offered him tea and gingerbread. Barclay made up a plate, anyway, and Dennis seemed hardly to realize Barclay had steered him into a chair and served him. Dennis picked up a fork absently. "Jane Chatham's gone missing."

"What?" Daisy glanced at her father. "She wasn't at home with Ralph when the storm hit?"

"I guess she was down at The Wedding Diner. I'm not sure. That's the last place Ralph said he knew she was. Doing inventory, he said."

"But if your jail got hit, and it's across the street from the diner," Robert began.

Dennis sipped his tea, hardly noticing Barclay hovering at his elbow. "The diner didn't get so much as a scratch."

"That's wonderful news!" Daisy felt a strange cramp hit her stomach, ignored it for the moment. Sipped some more tea, told herself it would pass.

"Anyway, she's not in the diner. I checked. So I came here because, frankly, Robert, I'm going to need to borrow your security detail to help us search."

"Fine. Barclay, give the boys a ring, will you? Have them come in to go with the sheriff."

Daisy looked at Dennis, worried. "I'm sure everyone has tried her cell phone, but of course some phone service is still out."

"That's what's making it tricky." Dennis shrugged. "If Jane was supposed to be in the diner doing inventory, and the building didn't get hit, I can't imagine why she's not there now."

"I don't know, but I'll take my truck and help search, too," Daisy said, and Dennis, her father and Barclay all said, "No!"

"Pardon me," Barclay said. "It's not like me to insert an opinion—"

"Never mind," Robert said. "Daisy, sweetheart, you're not leaving the house again. If I have to sit up all night playing chess and gin rummy with you to make sure you don't leave again, that's what I'll do."

The strange cramp slithered over her stomach again.

Daisy put a hand on her tummy. "More hands on deck means we find her faster."

"If I have the ranch crew, that'll be enough." Dennis stood. "Thanks, Robert."

"No problem. Take what you need. The hitch, the hauler, whatever."

"Just the manpower for now. Daisy, get your gang up, too. Tell 'em to meet me at the creek."

"Why the creek? What's going on at the creek all of a sudden?" She looked at Dennis. "I thought you said Jane was at the diner?" She felt another cramp. "John's down at the creek now."

"He is?" Dennis seemed stunned. "Why?"

"I have no idea. I didn't want to leave him there, but he insisted."

"Since when has someone insisted on something that you listened to?" Dennis demanded.

"I don't know. Motherhood must be softening me up."

"I'll say." Dennis whistled. "Or being a married woman has done it."

"I'm not married yet."

"Rumor on the grapevine is that it'll happen before frost hits the pumpkins." Dennis lifted his hat, and he disappeared down the hall. The front door opened, and they could hear the sounds of trucks revving up. She texted her gang to let them know the sheriff wanted them at the creek, then looked up to see her father smiling at her fondly.

"It does my heart good to see you so happy, Daisy girl."

"Happy about what?"

"Motherhood. Becoming a wife. It's what you always wanted more than anything."

It was true, not that she would admit that to anyone, not even her father. She was crazy in love with John, absolutely head over heels for him.

"I wish I'd been better to my wife." Robert sighed heavily, and Daisy started. Her father rarely talked about her mother, but Daisy remembered her mother as a soft, gentle, quiet soul. Very set apart from Robert, their marriage more formal than loving.

"Thing was, I got married early. We were young. I was full of hotheaded big plans for the world, everything I wanted to do. Put my marriage second. Last, really." He shook his head. "Should have been first, damn it."

"Oh, Dad." Daisy reached over, patted his arm. "Don't think about things like that."

"I just want you to have everything you want. Everyone always said you were a wild child, that I should rein you in. But I knew what your heart was, and that you dreamed of a home, a husband, children and to belong in this small, opinionated town." He laughed ruefully. "I wasn't much help with any of those goals, but now they're all within your reach. I think you've found the man for you."

She'd feel better when John returned, that was for sure. "I can't imagine where Jane is. I talked to Cosette earlier and I thought everything was fine."

Barclay hovered at her elbow. "I notice you keep rubbing your stomach, Miss Daisy. Are you feeling well? I could make you some warm milk—"

"I'm fine. I think I'll go to bed. Thank you, Barclay." Maybe if she went to her room, Barclay and her father would retire. There was no point in keeping them up just because she was worried about John. And Jane. And everything. Even the idea of a wedding was gnawing on her mind. The sheriff had said there'd be a wedding before frost was on the pumpkins, but that wasn't possible. She rubbed her stomach as she walked upstairs slowly. Each stair seemed to take longer than the last, with more effort needed, effort that seemed to drain her.

And then, just as she reached the landing, Daisy realized she was going to faint. She grabbed on to the balustrade and pulled herself up over the final stair, letting herself gently sink onto the floor safely before she gave in to the blackness.

Chapter Ten

"High-risk pregnancies are not uncommon with trip-lets," Dr. Costa said. "But you're young and healthy, so fortunately, I think there's a good chance you can carry the babies longer."

She'd been taken into Austin by ambulance. She was embarrassed for taking up all the manpower and re-sources when help was needed in Bridesmaids Creek. On the other hand, it'd been so scary when she'd real-ized she was blacking out and falling that she was glad she was here and getting medical assistance.

"What happened?" she asked, her voice sounding weak even to her. John glanced at her, concerned, her hand held tightly in his.

"Three babies are a lot on your system, basically. We're running tests to find out more, but I suspect low blood sugar, maybe some anemia."

"I've always been extremely healthy," Daisy pro-tested. "And I'd been eating gingerbread and drinking tea. I don't think I could have had low blood sugar, Dr. Costa, I really don't."

"We'll see. It's just my initial guess. Now that we have you stabilized, we'll just let you lie here and rest for a while."

"How long?"

"Maybe a week." He didn't glance up from his chart. "We're going to run tests on the babies, as well, to make certain there isn't anything wrong with the pregnancy—"

She felt the blood turn cold in her face and arms. Hopefully there was nothing wrong with her precious babies.

"Did anyone find Jane?"

"I did." John rubbed her hand. "Don't worry about anything. BC's still going to be there when you get back. Right now, you just need to rest."

Daisy felt herself getting sleepy against her will. "Where'd you find her?"

"Don't worry. Everything will be fine."

Her eyes snapped open. "That's why you went to the creek, wasn't it?" she asked groggily. "You were looking for Jane."

"Go to sleep, babe."

"But we never made love," she said, whispering because it was so extremely difficult to speak. "I wanted to make love to you."

"Shh, babe," he whispered. "Everything's going to be fine."

She closed her eyes, letting her cowboy soothe her, wishing she could stay awake and tell him how much he meant to her. How sorry she was that she'd made him chase her like crazy for so long. She'd known all along that John adored her, and foolishly, she'd ignored what he was offering.

Like her father, she completely understood what it meant to have regrets.

Sam walked in looking concerned, his arms full of

a big white teddy bear. "No worries, the cavalry has arrived."

"Cavalry?" John raised a brow.

"Indeed." Sam kissed Daisy on the cheek, shook John's hand. "When I heard Daisy would be laid up for a while, I knew you needed my presence."

"How so?" John asked.

Sam set the bear down and grinned. "Because I've never let a brother down yet. And while you weren't looking, I became ordained to perform weddings. Ordained via the internet, but that suffices here in Texas." He seemed really happy to report his new standing. "It's the least I can do, considering that I once offered to marry Daisy myself. And if I don't do it, you're going to end up with children and no wife, John."

"Daisy and I will get married soon enough," John said, but he sounded hesitant.

He glanced toward her, as did Sam.

"Don't look at me. I can't even think about a wedding right now." Daisy was adamant.

"Hmm." John seemed to consider Sam's words. "You *have* given me the slip once before."

"Yes, but—"

"Actually, if you think about it, she's given you the slip several times." Sam flung himself in a chair, delighted to be stoking trouble. "Let's see, first there was—"

"Never mind. Let me see this license of yours." John waited for him to produce it. "I'm assuming that if you're here, it's because you think your services are required."

Daisy felt like she'd been tossed into a whirlwind.

"Hang on a minute. There's too much going on to even think about a wedding!"

"What's going on?" John asked, and she thought he sounded a bit wary.

"Well, Bridesmaids Creek for one." Daisy swallowed. "How could we even think about getting married when Jane is missing—"

"I found her and took her home last night," John reminded her.

"Okay, but the jail is gone and the Haunted H, too. And there's damage to a lot of homes. It seems selfish to get married when our friends are suffering," Daisy said, floundering. How could she explain that she didn't want to get married while she was bed bound? Was that vain? She wanted what the other brides in Bridesmaids Creek had gotten: the full hometown wedding with family and friends.

"Actually it's not selfish at all. It's being very considerate," Sam said, throwing in his two cents like the trickster he was. "After all, you need to be married for the sake of the babies, I should think. And there's so much turmoil in town that your marrying out of town, sort of like an elopement, in fact, exactly like an elopement, would keep everyone from feeling compelled to drop everything and do their wedding duties."

"That's true…" Daisy saw the good sense in what Sam was saying. It was a guaranteed fact that as soon as everyone heard that there was going to be a wedding, everyone would cease everything they were doing to help her out. Weddings weren't done small in Bridesmaids Creek.

It was something she'd always wanted, though. The big wedding for Daisy Donovan, once the town's bad girl, making good, finally. Acceptance was a dream very near to her heart.

"How legal is this stupid internet ordination you've gotten?" John sounded like he was almost growling, probably not pleased that Sam was ramrodding this new twist.

Yet Sam's plan had a lot of merit—this time.

"Oh, it's all very legal," he said cheerfully. "I worked real hard to obtain my certification, because I figured you two might mess around long enough that you might need some kind of emergency bell-ringing."

"That's just not really funny." John definitely sounded like he was growling now. Daisy glanced at him, surprised.

"Why do you act like you want to gnaw his head off?" she asked the man who suddenly didn't sound very much as if he wanted to become a husband.

"Never mind." John shrugged. "It's up to Daisy."

She stared at him. "That's it? It's up to me?"

He shrugged again. "Of course. As Sam said, you've left me at the altar before. And I recall telling you that you'd have to ask me to marry you, since you've been notably reluctant to race to the altar with me."

Drat. She'd forgotten that he'd wanted a clear green light from her this time.

Daisy swallowed, suddenly aware that she'd been expecting John to make all the sacrifices in their relationship. "Here's the thing. I don't really want to get married like this, John."

"Like what?" His brown eyes hooded a bit, the muscles of his broad chest stiffening with tension, preparing himself for bad news.

"In the hospital, for starters. By Sam, no offense,"

she said quickly to Sam. "But not with an internet-earned diploma of some kind." She looked at her maybe-soon-to-be husband. "You know very well we have no reason to expect that it's valid."

"It is," Sam said.

"Excuse me," Daisy said quickly, "but I have some experience with men with an agenda. My father for starters, my gang for further illustration of my point. And you're definitely a typical guy who likes to move people around like puzzle pieces. You've been doing it since you came to Bridesmaids Creek."

"Hey!" Sam yelped. "I resemble that remark!"

"Yes, you do." Daisy frowned at him. "What I've noticed is that you manipulate people into doing what you want them to do—"

"I *help* them," Sam emphasized. "The spirit is pure."

"And what you usually want someone to do is get married," Daisy went on, "yet I notice you never, ever date anyone yourself. Why is that?"

"Yeah, Sam, why is that?" John laughed. "Daisy's made several good points."

Sam sighed, pulled the big white bear into his lap. "Is it wrong for a fellow to want his friends to be happy? The same friends that came here looking for brides? Looking for love?"

"I'll let you officiate a ceremony for us, Sam, when you've gone out on a real date. So you better make it snappy. These babies may not be content to stay put until the end of time. Which is exactly how long I suspect you were planning on going without dating a living, breathing woman."

Sam shook his head. "Greatness can't be rushed."

"Neither can mediocrity. Laziness." Daisy settled back against the pillow.

"You've figured me out, then. When it comes to love, I'm lazy. I admit it. Relationships are too damn much work. And I don't think I'm cut out for henpeckery."

Daisy laughed. "I don't henpeck John."

"Yeah." Sam glowered at his buddy. "But only because you respect a man who can shoot the head off a nail. Who's going to respect me?"

"Handsome Sam?" John grinned. "Everyone respects Handsome Sam."

"No, they don't." His face was woebegone. "If they respected me, they wouldn't be talking about my looks. They'd be talking about my deeds."

"That's the most pathetic, pitiful bit of sorry-for-myself I've ever heard," Daisy said. "You're trying to make me feel bad about not letting you use your piece of paper that's so new the ink is still wet on it to officiate our ceremony."

"Yeah, I am. Is it working?" Sam peered at her.

"No. I'm not getting married here. I'm not getting married in a hurry, by a man who printed a fake license from his computer so he could claim he was certified to get John and me to say we do!"

"Damn shame, that." Sam leaned back in the chair, closed his eyes. "Then again, I'll take a nap and let you lovebirds talk it over. I'm sure there'll be plenty of back-chat to be said over the matter."

"There's not going to be any backchat!" Daisy wished she could get out of the bed and go home where she didn't feel so powerless. Here she was connected to tubes and monitors. She'd been rushed here without her typical clothes, didn't even have a hairbrush. John had done his best to pack for her, but what man knew what a woman needed in her overnight bag? Barclay had tried to help, apparently, but John had waved him off in his great hurry to follow the ambulance to Austin.

She'd been charmed by John's desire to take care of her himself. She smiled as Sam began to snore lightly. "It's him, not you."

John winked. "I know, beautiful. Trust me, I know. A little of my buddy goes a long way."

"He is right, though." She hadn't expected to find herself off her feet so soon. "But I can't think about getting married when I'm worried about the babies. I don't think I've ever been so scared as when I woke up and found myself being carted off into an ambulance."

"I completely understand." He came over to sit on the bed next to her, leaned her head against his shoulder. "It's all going to work out."

"I hope so."

"It is." His voice was strong with determination. "You know what we should do?"

"Let Sam perform the ceremony his way, and do it our way later? Just to cover all the bases?"

"I was going to say get a cup of warm water and put his hand in it to see if we can make him pee himself," John said, "but yeah, your plan works, too."

"The warm water idea is definitely intriguing." Daisy looked up at him. "He drove all the way here to see us, he bought the babies a bear, he claims he somehow got himself ordained just for us, and we want to put his hand in a cup of warm water. Is that wrong?"

John laughed. "It's so right that it's hard to believe I'm not going to do it."

"Softy."

"Me! You're the one who wants to let him use his faux piece of paper so he can brag about being the one who got us married."

"Yeah." Daisy slowly nodded. "When you put it like that, it doesn't sound so silly."

"No, it doesn't."

They sat quietly for a few minutes, and John kissed her hand. Brushed her knuckles with his lips. Daisy looked at their sleeping lump of a friend, who was good-hearted in spite of his prankster ways, remembered that this man had served overseas with her husband.

"I just wonder if it might be good for your friendship to allow Sam to have his moment in the sun," Daisy said.

"I don't want you to do anything you'll regret later. And it might be just as exciting to do the warm water trick. At least from your perspective."

Daisy looked at Sam. "It was sweet of him to try to play Madame Matchmaker's role."

"Those two are in cahoots, along with Jane. Don't feel too sentimental for him."

Daisy looked at John. "Are you sure?"

"Sure as I'm breathing."

She smiled. "All of you who came here for Ty are no stranger to trying to finagle your way to what you want. You, Sam, Cisco, Justin, even Ty. You're brothers in schemes."

"I'll tell you a secret. We didn't really come here to find brides. I know that's the line in BC, but honestly, that was sort of window dressing."

Daisy was astonished. "But that's all any of you have done, try to march each other to the altar. You've competed in the Bridesmaids Creek swim and the Best

Man's Fork run, egging each other out of bachelor status!"

"I know." He grinned. "We were okay with that rumor going around. After a while, it sort of became rural legend, and we were okay with that, too. But the truth is, we only came here to support Ty Spurlock because we could tell he needed help."

Daisy thought back. Justin Morant had come to Bridesmaids Creek first, meeting Mackenzie Hawthorne and her four little baby girls, falling head over boots in love with all of them. Then Ty had gotten caught in his own trap and fallen for Jade Harper, which still amused all of BC, because he was supposedly shepherding his brothers-in-arms to the altar. Cisco Grant went down hard for Suz Hawthorne—and that had left John and Handsome Sam as the last bachelors standing among the group Ty had brought to town with the intention of growing Bridesmaids Creek. "What kind of help?"

"We could tell he was worried about how stuff was going around here. Frankly, at the time, your father wasn't doing a whole lot to help out."

"That's true," Daisy murmured, feeling horribly guilty about the part she'd played in all that, too.

He tightened his arms around her as if he could tell what was she thinking, absolutely wouldn't let her have any regrets.

"So Ty felt like we could help out around the town. At the time, he talked about odd jobs and stuff. Working around both the Hanging H Ranch and the Haunted H year-round Halloween attraction. We liked the thought of being outdoors, and the town sounded cool. The idea of living in a family oriented kind of place was appealing to all of us. So, Sam, Cisco and I decided to head here, at least for a couple of months. BC grows on you, though, and now it's been a few years."

Where might John have gone otherwise? He clearly had no desire to live the same way his parents and brothers did, even though their lifestyle certainly suited them. "I'm glad you came to BC."

"It goes without saying that I am, too."

She looked at Sam, who was snoring like crazy. "So what about Sam? Has he ever dated anyone?"

"Not that we know of. Not since we've known him, anyway."

"Poor Sam!"

"Don't feel sorry for him. He says he's too busy. I don't know with what, but he says he is."

"So he just works at the Hanging H, and becomes a doting uncle to all the babies his SEAL brothers have?"

"I guess."

Daisy took a deep breath. "We're going to have to do it."

"Put his hand in warm water while he's snoring?"

"No. We're going to have to let him officiate our wedding."

John pulled away slightly to look at her. "Are you sure you don't want to do the water trick instead?"

"I'm sure." She gazed at Sam, the big bear of a man collapsed in the chair like a tired doll. "He put a lot of thought into this. We can't let him down."

"So you're asking me to marry you?"

She turned to face him, stared deep into his eyes. "Yes. I am asking you to marry me. When our snoring friend awakens, would you, John Lopez 'Squint' Mathison, do me the great honor of becoming my sexy, handsome husband?"

Chapter Eleven

"I accept," John stated in a hurry, before she could take her sudden proposal back. "Sam, get up off your duff! You've got a job to do."

Sam blinked his eyes sleepily, then jackknifed to a sitting position. "Is there a raid? What's happening?" He looked around wildly. John realized he was probably searching for his firearm and primed to hit the ground running.

"Easy, brother. We're in Austin," John said softly, and Sam relaxed as if someone had pulled the air out of him. His brown hair was stood on end, but John could almost hear his blood pressure calming. "Didn't mean to scare the hell out of you."

"Man, I don't know. Guess I was dreaming." Sam looked at Daisy, who wore the cutest expression of alarm. "Sorry, Daisy."

"It's fine. John should be more delicate when he disturbs you."

Sam rose, his face returning to the teasing expression they all knew so well. Cagily, he said, "So now that I'm awake, am I performing ministerial duties?"

"Is that really all you came here for?" John demanded.

"I came to see Daisy, and to bring the impending

bundles of joy their first present from Uncle Handsome Sam."

Daisy laughed, but John scowled. "Daisy's asked me to marry her." He said it with pride.

"That's awesome!" Sam laughed. "I hope you don't regret it, beautiful. I swear I'm the better man," he teased, going to kiss Daisy's cheek. John pulled him back when he deemed Sam was being just a bit too attentive.

"That's enough. Easy, Romeo."

Sam looked at Daisy. "You don't have to marry him, you know. I'd do the honors in a heartbeat."

John sighed. "You don't even want to get married."

"No, but I can make an exception in this case."

"That's enough. You have a wedding to perform, and it's not your own."

"And perform it I will!" Sam rubbed his hands together. "We don't have a second to spare."

"Well, actually," Daisy said, "we need to spare a few moments."

John put up his hands. "You asked, I accepted, we have a willing pastor to officiate. Don't slow us down, Daisy. We're over the hump here."

"And it wasn't easy getting over that hump," Daisy agreed. "But we can do a lot of good with our marriage, if we play our cards right."

John sank into a chair, stared at the woman he couldn't quite seem to catch. "Let's skip playing cards and just get married already."

"The thing is, we need to do this right. To do it right, we need Madame Matchmaker."

"We're already matched. She's had her hands in our relationship up to her elbows. Maybe not as much as she would have liked, but enough." John was eager to get the "I do's" said.

"Not necessarily," Sam said, and John frowned.

"Whose side are you on? You do realize this woman has eluded me for years? Do you really want to give her a reason to get away from me again?" John demanded.

"Here's the thing," Daisy said, ignoring the good-natured ribbing between the men. Sometimes it didn't sound good-natured, but she knew they had a relationship that went deeper than any silly argument. That was the thing about Daisy, the more time went on, the more comfortable he felt around her. Not too comfortable, of course—he still wanted to make love to her wildly day and night, as they had in Montana. But he felt comfortable with her.

She made him smile in a way he'd once wondered if he'd ever smile again.

"Cosette, our illustrious matchmaker, believes her magic has deserted her." Daisy looked at the men. "This is a golden opportunity to help her get her mojo back."

"Oh, no." John shook his head. "I'm not waiting for Cosette's magic. I've got three little babies who are going to wear my name from the second their eyes open in this world. Plus, if you recall, she had your gang tie me to a tree during the last race. No, I'm not waiting on Cosette."

"I see where you're going with this," Sam said to Daisy, and John wondered if telling his buddy to butt out would be a foolhardy thing to do. It was Sam and his new freestyle ordination who just about had Daisy to "I do," so John contented himself with gazing at his lovely bride-to-be-as-soon-as-he-could-manage-it and waited for Sam's epiphany to reveal itself.

"If Cosette believes you two are together and getting married because of her matchmaking skills, then she'll feel like her magic hasn't deserted her." Sam looked pleased. "It's two for the price of one."

John didn't like the sound of that. There was already one more attending this marriage proposal than necessary. Again, he reminded himself that his buddy had his back, so he kept silent.

"We get Cosette's magic to recharge her belief in herself, and Bridesmaids Creek comes back to life." Sam nodded wisely at Daisy. "People don't always see your good side, Daisy Donovan, but you definitely have some angel running strong in you. Sexy angel, too," he said with a flourish, and John said, "Hey!" as sternly as he could manage it, secretly grateful that Sam was saying nice things about Daisy because she deserved it.

"Thank you." Daisy sounded happy, and John forgave his buddy all his interruptions and interferences on the spot. Just to hear someone else acknowledge what he himself had always seen in the brunette stunner made him realize all over again why he'd allowed Sam into his tight-knit circle of brothers in the first place.

"Thanks," John said softly.

"No thanks needed." Sam began scrolling through his phone. "Now, we need a bouquet, and maybe a veil?" He looked at Daisy. "Do you want to call Cosette or shall I?"

"But we haven't decided how to do this, have we?" Daisy was so adorable as she sat in the hospital bed, looking worried about Cosette, that John fell in love with her all over again.

"One of us is going to tell Cosette that you and John can't get married because he believes your marriage won't last since the Bridesmaids Creek charms have failed for you. If you recall, none of your three chances at the magic ever pointed to John being the man of your dreams. The prince of your heart, as it were." Sam looked quite pleased with his plan.

"Hell, no, we're not telling Cosette that! Don't stir up that BC magic nonsense," John said.

Daisy gasped, and Sam looked chagrined. John realized he'd stepped in it big-time. "Oh, come on. It's just superstition. You know that, right?"

"And you've always been superstitious as hell," Sam said. "You know *that*, right?"

Daisy's expression was still steeped in anxiety. John tried to look like a man who'd just been proposed to. "In the real world, the world outside of BC, not everybody jumps around to the tune of busybodies. Cute little busybodies, but busybodies with an agenda just the same."

Daisy looked like she might cry.

"May I just remind you, brother, that Madame Matchmaker said, and I repeat, 'there will be no wedding in BC for you?', as a result of your unsuccessful attempts in the Bridesmaids Creek swim and the Best Man's Fork run?" Sam looked disgusted. "What SEAL gets a leg cramp during arguably the most important swim of his life?"

"First of all," John said, "going back to my original point, those were not the most important missions in my life. I can think of a few swims we did in very dire parts of the world, my friend, and you can, too, wherein my leg did not cramp up, nor did my shooting skills."

Daisy's eyes filled with tears. Sam cleared his throat.

"Oh, hell. I'm not being very romantic, am I?" John crumpled into his chair. "Daisy, I'm sorry. Sorry as heck." He pushed his hat back, shook his head. Pointed at Sam. "You are causing trouble, buddy."

Sam looked innocent. "Your lack of romance is not my fault!"

He snorted. "One day, Sam Barr, some little lady is going to decide she wants to pin you down, and all of us are going to eat popcorn and watch with smiles on our faces."

Sam's face contorted from astonished to concerned. "Dude, that's a horrible curse to lay on a brother! It's bad, really bad. Friends don't put that on friends."

"Anyway," Daisy said, "getting back to Cosette, if you don't want to go with the local customs, that's a decision I leave up to you." She looked at John, her dark eyes a little sad, and his heart felt as if it sank to his boots.

"Absolutely not. I let my pigheaded mouth get the best of me." He manned up big-time, determined to make Daisy happy. "I'll call Cosette myself."

Daisy looked pleased, and Sam appeared relieved.

"Thank you," Daisy said, and John felt better.

"I knew you'd want to do this right. Any man would want to redeem himself after the leg cramp episode," Sam said.

"You know, I wish we had put your hand in a glass of warm water while you napped," John groused, and Daisy laughed, and Sam postured as if he wasn't worried but he knew very well anything was possible.

John grinned at Daisy and pulled out his phone. "Let's get this party started. What do I tell our illustrious matchmaker?"

"I'm afraid I don't know," Cosette said when John called her a half hour later with a well-prepared script he'd been given by Daisy.

He hoped he could pull off the magic.

"*You* don't know what to do?" John said, when Cosette paused.

"It's not a matter of you and Daisy getting married," Cosette told him. "But as far as the magic goes, I'm afraid I don't have any pull."

"You don't have any pull?" Beside him, Daisy's face went a little pale. He had to fix this—and fast. "How can you not have any pull? You pull everyone's strings in BC!"

"Yes, but you see, I'm divorced now. I'm on my own. If I can't make my own match work, how can I make a match for anyone else?"

John swallowed hard. "Cosette, you know that you and Phillipe are meant to be together like salt and pepper. Marriage isn't the only bond between you."

"Maybe not. But to be honest, I started losing a bit of faith when Mackenzie Hawthorne's first marriage hit the skids. Though, to be sure, her first husband was a weasel. She should never have married him."

"So you're saying that the magic makes mistakes?" John was trying very hard to see through the fog of superstition BC layered over itself.

"I made a mistake." Cosette took a moment to compose her thoughts. "The magic never does. But my confidence really ebbed a little. Up until then, I had a perfect record, and Phillipe was Monsieur Unmatchmaker in name only. He had no job, except for tutoring, of course. But no matches to unmake. We never needed that service."

John's head swam. "It's okay, Cosette. Ty Spurlock said that Mackenzie's first marriage really hadn't been prodded along by you but by him."

"Oh, what does Ty know?" she asked huffily, but he thought he heard hope in her voice. "Anyway, what do you possibly think I can do for Daisy? No one gets more than three chances at the magic. It's just not possible."

"So what would happen if we get married without assistance from Bridesmaids Creek magic?"

Daisy's eyes went huge. She'd been listening attentively this whole time, but now she looked positively stunned. John decided right then and there that nothing was going to keep him from giving her the thing she'd been dreaming of all her life.

"You'd just get married," Cosette said. "Nothing happens at all."

He hesitated. That didn't sound right. Something had to happen—this was Bridesmaids Creek. Everyone was always in a stew about the magic.

"So do I take that to mean that you and Daisy have agreed to get married?" Cosette asked.

"We certainly would like to. But as you know, our getting to the altar has been—"

"Difficult. Strewn with rocks. I know," Cosette said, and he glanced at Daisy again. She looked as if her heart was in her eyes and in danger of melting away. "And you want it to work out between the two of you, anyway."

"More than anything."

Cosette was quiet for a minute. Then she said, "Do you remember the night we took you to the cavern?"

"Yes. I do. I found Jane Chatham there that night after the storm."

"Then that's all you need to know. Give Daisy my love. She's such a sweet girl, you know. Always has been. Although I'm putting good money on the fact that those three boys of hers are going to be rootin' tootin' rascals."

She hung up, leaving John wondering what the hell had just happened.

"What did she say?" Daisy asked eagerly. Sam remained motionless in his chair, his gaze hooded, waiting for the big pronouncement.

John couldn't talk about the cave. It was secret, sacrosanct. There was nothing to tell, anyway, because he didn't know what he was supposed to have seen that night. It had been a wonderful underground place, nothing more. A hidden part of BC no one knew about. When Jane had misplaced herself after the blowout storm that had hit BC, he'd had a hunch and gone looking for her there. Sure enough, he'd located her at the mouth of the cave, but he hadn't gone in it a second time. He hadn't asked her what she'd been up to, and she hadn't offered any information. With the town devastated the way it had been that night, he'd been only too happy to grab her, then call around to let everyone know he'd found Jane.

The cave wasn't his secret to share. He had no idea why Cosette brought it up now. He looked at Daisy, the woman he hungered for, the woman who'd driven him mad with desire and love and all the wonderful emotions a man needed to feel about a woman.

He wasn't letting her get away. Not if he could help it.

"It's okay if we get married," John said.

"Okay?"

He nodded. "Cosette said nothing will happen if we get married."

"That's the point. Nothing will happen." Daisy looked worried. "The magic won't happen."

His heart curled up a little as some concern sank in, but he couldn't deny Daisy's words. "I had a funny feeling that's where Cosette was going with that."

"So basically you have to fix this on your own," Sam stated. "Wouldn't it have been better if you hadn't gotten a leg cramp in the first place?" He laughed, and John told himself he was going to turn his buddy into a pretzel if he didn't hush up and quit stirring up trouble.

"It's not all his fault," Daisy said.

"It's not?" Sam asked.

"No. It's not." She looked at John. "I deliberately didn't win him in the second race. When I saw him on the banks instead of Cisco, I slowed down. Probably in the last fifty, I definitely wasn't swimming faster than Suz."

"You slowed down on purpose?" So this was heartbreak. He'd always suspected—everyone had always suspected—Daisy hadn't swum lights-out once she'd realized he was the prize, but it was still hard to hear coming from the only woman he'd ever wanted to win.

"And then Cisco nullified the third race by winning and declaring himself already married," Sam said. "That was a day that really set BC on its ear. The big dummy." He sounded vastly amused by that.

"I don't need the magic, John. I don't think it exists for me, or ever will, no matter what we do."

He studied Daisy. He could hear the despair in her voice. "Cosette didn't seem all that hopeful."

"That's that, then." Daisy's shoulders slumped. "Sam, you might as well go ahead and marry us. This way, at least it's done. The babies will have their father's name at birth, and I'll—"

John held his breath. "You'll what?"

"I'll be married." Daisy looked at him, and she smiled, but it didn't look like a smile. More like a determination. A vow, to do the right thing.

He didn't want to be the right thing. Hell, he never had been in his life. Why should he start now?

"Nope," John said. "There'll be no wedding today."

"What?" Sam demanded. "Listen, buddy, I don't know if you heard, but your bride actually said she'd accept your dumb ass. If I was you, I'd hop on that offer."

John grinned, suddenly feeling on top of the world again. "Can't do it." He leaned down, dropped a kiss on Daisy that turned sexy in a heartbeat. Oh, his girl liked him fine. She wanted to marry him.

She just wanted the magic, too.

He was fine with that.

After all, there wasn't a prince in fairy-tale land that had ever stumbled upon his princess without having to go on an enchanted win-your-lady grail first.

And if there was one thing he'd always been good at, it was life on the move.

Chapter Twelve

John got Daisy home under strict instructions from the doctor, who said she wasn't to move. She had to stay on medication to keep the babies "in as long as possible," which nearly gave John heart failure. Any man would be frightened by that kind of talk.

And they still weren't married. He didn't know how he was going to manage that trick.

"You lie right here and don't move. Not a muscle," John said, ensconcing her in a downstairs bedroom in the main house at the Donovan compound.

Daisy looked up at him. "I can't stand being away from all the action. I'll go mad in here."

Barclay cleared his throat, and Robert shuffled from foot to foot nervously. Daisy's gang had all crowded into the room, too, trying to be part of the welcome-home committee.

"We could make a place for her in the den, which is closer to the kitchen and living room," Barclay suggested. "Miss Daisy has always needed to be close by the action."

"And it would be easier to keep an eye on her," Robert added.

John decided he needed to give in gracefully. "But no excitement. I leave you in charge," he told Barclay.

"I'll see that she doesn't leave the sofa bed."

John felt that Barclay's word was probably as close to gold as anyone's could be. And Robert looked as if he was probably going to turn out to be quite a hoverer. "Okay, den it is. But the doctor scared the bejesus out of me, babe. You and I are going on autopilot until my sons are born."

"We'll all help," Carson Dare said.

John thought that for once he was probably grateful for Daisy's band of rowdies. If nothing else, they were loyal, and he valued loyalty and brotherhood. "We'll take all the help we can get. You have to arrange all of that with Barclay, though," he said, belatedly realizing he might be stepping on the butler's domain. And Robert's, too, for that matter.

"I'm going to head out for a bit. I need to check in at the Hanging H. Are you going to be okay, babe?" he asked Daisy.

"Do I look like these guys would let me be anything but?" Daisy asked, smiling.

She was the center of attention, which she loved more than anything. John grinned. "Call me if you need anything."

"Take your time," she said sweetly, and later on John would remember that his best girl had said that.

He should have taken heed.

DAISY GOT ON the phone with Cosette as soon as John departed. She'd shooed everyone else away, too, claiming she needed a nap.

But she had way too much to do.

"Cosette, I'm ready," she said when her friend picked up the phone.

"Ready for what?"

"Ready to start training as your apprentice."

Cosette didn't laugh. "Are you sure?"

If there was anything Cosette needed to get her groove back, it was someone to mentor—at least that was the conclusion Daisy had come to.

She was pretty sure she'd hit on a winning idea. If she was right, she'd get everything she'd ever dreamed of.

"Of course I'm sure. If you don't accept me as an apprentice, how am I ever going to learn?"

"I do need help," Cosette said, her voice quavering a bit. "However, I'm not sure I'll make all that good of a teacher. My magic wand no longer has any spark."

"We'll worry about the wand later. We have to get cracking on this project. Otherwise, Bridesmaids Creek is going to really lack for marriage matches. Think about that for a minute."

"It's too horrible to contemplate!"

"I know. The guys meant well with their dating service idea. Whoever heard of a cigar bar in a matchmaking establishment?"

"Not me," Cosette said, her voice a little unsteady.

Daisy took a deep breath. If it was the last thing she did, she was going to get Cosette and Phillipe back in their old establishment. She should never have sided with her father on taking over those spaces. "Okay, then. The doctor has me on bed rest, so I can't move. You're going to have to teach me by phone."

"I can do that. But I may drop by, just to make sure everything's sticking."

"Even better. If you have time, that is."

"My dear, I always have time to take on an apprentice. My first! This is a happy day!"

"I'll try not to let you down."

"Impossible! Who's our first victim?"

"I'll tell you when you get here."

She hung up, smiled when her father came in the room.

"How are you feeling?" Robert asked.

"Like a million bucks. I'm going to be Cosette's new matchmaking apprentice."

Robert hesitated, then grinned. "Who are you practicing on first?"

"What if I said it was you?"

He shook his head vehemently. "Absolutely not. I was a terrible husband."

Daisy took that in. "Then we'll start with Carson Dare."

"He's been in love with you forever. Won't he be a tough nut to crack?"

"It'll be a good test of my skills. If I can get Carson matched, the rest should fall in line."

"I don't know," Robert said, sounding worried. "This could backfire."

"It could," Daisy said, "but it won't."

WHEN JOHN RETURNED, he was surprised to find Cosette and Daisy peering at some kind of flowchart and what looked like pieces of paper they'd tossed in a frilly pink hat with a huge red feather on it.

"Hello, Cosette. Daisy, darling, shouldn't you be resting, beautiful?" He realized they were paying him little attention beyond a cursory greeting. "So I'll just go find your father, okay?"

"Dad would love that." Daisy favored him with a

huge smile, and John felt a warm glow run all over him. Okay, he was good and smitten, and she wasn't going to listen to him about relaxing, anyway.

Even he'd known that was going to be the impossible dream. Daisy'd always had too much energy to just sit on a sofa and nest like a bird. He was going to have to ease off a little.

He went and found Robert hanging out in the kitchen. "Evening."

Robert nodded. "How is everything in town?"

"Slowly getting put back together." He glanced back toward the garden room. "How long has Cosette been here?"

"Thirty minutes." He shrugged. "I think they're planning the nursery."

With a hat with a huge feather on it straight out of Cosette's eccentric closet? "I don't think that's what the girls have up their sleeves."

Robert poured him a whiskey. "Well, then, it's probably nothing we need to be involved in."

"That's it? You're going to cave that easily?" John was dying to know what the ladies were up to. He had a feeling his wife-to-be was getting into something more exciting than she should be for a woman who was supposed to be on strict bed rest. "Cheers," he said, lifting his glass to Robert. "I'm going to head back and check on them for a second."

"You do that. I'll be here." Robert stared moodily at a map of the town, but John decided he'd worry about that later. Back in the garden room, the ladies gave him a quick glance and went back to their flowchart, which appeared to be filling out nicely.

He had an uneasy feeling about what was going on here.

"Daisy, babe, is there something I can help you ladies with?"

"I don't think so, darling. Unless you want to become an apprentice to Monsieur Unmatchmaker, in which case we would have a lot to do together! Wouldn't that be fun?"

He hesitated, caught by Daisy's bright smile. God, he loved it when she smiled like that. "I'm sorry, sweetheart. Become a what kind of apprentice?"

"I'm working with Cosette now."

He sank into a chair. "You're going to become a matchmaker?"

"Yes, I am." She smiled so proudly he felt himself get hard, which caught him by surprise. It was Daisy, everything about her, that made his heart fire up in his chest and burn like red-hot coals. He adored her, he loved her and he had absolutely zero desire to become Monsieur Unmatchmaker the Second, learning the ropes of BC from Phillipe. And then one day ending up chanting and practicing yoga with strings of beads hanging from every doorway and incense permeating his domicile.

"Don't worry. I can do this and rest, too," Daisy told him. "Cosette and I think you're the perfect man to become Phillipe's apprentice."

He swallowed hard. Stared at that bright smile. Told himself that sometimes a man just did what he had to do to win the fair damsel.

"I'm really better with rodeo. Stuff like that," he said. "I'm a traveling man. I don't think I know much about marriages. Or un-marriages. I've got enough trouble trying to figure out how to get my own bride to the altar."

"It's just a different kind of race." Cosette smiled at him. "You see what I mean?"

He held his breath, not wanting Daisy's smile to disappear. They were hardly asking him to sit in the desert and pray he didn't get nailed by enemy sniper fire. "Not really, but I guess I could give it a shot. I mean, what the hell, right?"

Daisy beamed. "We'll make a great team."

He loved the sound of that. "Sure. Of course we will."

"So I'll tell Phillipe it's all set." Cosette rose. "In the meantime, you work on those matches, Daisy. It'll be your first test. I just know you're going to do wonderfully!"

Daisy's smile could have lit the sun. "Thanks, Cosette. It means a lot to me."

He got it suddenly: this was the pinnacle of Daisy's dreams. Far from being the town bad girl, she'd be the woman to whom Cosette passed the mythical magic wand.

Damn, it was a lot to live up to. He was proud of her, and scared as hell for himself.

He knew nothing, and wanted to know nothing, about what an Unmatchmaker did. All he wanted was to be a different kind of family from the one he'd grown up in, set in reality and grounded in practicality, in one place, one home, or at least only moving when they wanted to, not when the rodeo circuit moved on. Not when the military said it was time to move.

"I'll walk Cosette to the door, doll face."

"Thank you. Good night, Cosette."

Cosette flopped a hand Daisy's way. "I'll be back tomorrow to check your progress."

"Cosette," he said, his voice low as they walked to the front door, "I'm not sure about this."

"You'll be fine. Phillipe specifically mentioned you by name."

"Me? Why me?" John couldn't have been more astounded. "I don't even know what he does."

Cosette patted his shoulder as she went out the door. "Did you find what you were looking for tonight?"

"You mean when I went to the cave? No, I didn't. I'm not sure what I'm looking for. You keep hinting that that's where I'll find answers, but I don't think so somehow."

"Where do you think the answers are?" She gazed up at him curiously.

He stared down at the pink-frosted-haired woman watching him patiently. Like a benevolent grandmother but with a spicy and unpredictable twist. "All I know is that I'm in love with Daisy, I have been forever, she's having my children and I want to marry her. You're supposed to be the keeper of the magic flame on that topic."

"I'm teaching everything I know to Daisy. Much good may an old matchmaker's wand do her." Cosette sighed, downcast.

This wasn't good. John and Daisy needed a matchmaker with spark. Wasn't that why they were going through the charade of Daisy becoming a matchmaker's apprentice, and he apparently now would become an unmatchmaker's apprentice? To put the mystical spark back into Cosette, make her believe in herself again?

Once a long time ago, he'd taken a helluva fall from a bull. His head had hurt for ages, and he'd felt as if his brain wanted to come unglued from his cranium. The doctor had said he had a concussion, but it felt more like a devil's rock band playing in his skull. Time had been the healer, but time couldn't be rushed. Worse, he'd lost his faith in his skills, and the confidence that a man needed to face the depth of his worst fears and challenge himself.

After he'd recovered he'd gone into the military and learned quickly that a concussion was better than getting one's body parts blown off. He'd learned to hang on, stay focused, develop extra senses.

That was the place Cosette had to reach. Back in the saddle, back on her horse, dispensing fairy tales and magic with grandmotherly dynamism.

"I'm going to marry Daisy."

"I know you are." Cosette looked surprised. "I told you before, you don't need me for that."

"But Daisy wants a wedding that you've dredged up from the mysteries of your eccentric little BC-beating heart."

She pursed her lips, disgusted. "Is that any way to talk to a matchmaker?"

"I'm too desperate to mind the niceties. Cosette, you've got to fire up your skills one last time. Daisy needs you. *I* need you."

She looked doubtful. "It has to come from you." She tapped his chest, and John felt light-headed. Then stronger. Cosette gazed at him closely. "Everything you need is right here. It always was. Even when your parents took you from town to town, you were learning the things you needed to know. What did living on the road teach you?"

"To appreciate constancy. And variety. And people. Most of all, people. Everywhere we went, I met the most amazing people. I've met jugglers, puppeteers, ventriloquists, men who could fiddle like mad and women who could raise hell and a family at the same time."

"So, everything you see in Daisy."

"I hadn't thought of that, but yeah. She's amazing."

"So the answer will come to you. You can't rush the answer. Inspiration is the magic."

She floated out the door and John escorted her to her car. "Thanks for coming by. I know it means a lot to Daisy. And me."

"I know. It will all work out." She drove off, and John went to find Daisy.

Daisy waved him over. "See—my first victim is Carson. I've got just the woman for him."

John eyed the hat, which still contained several slips of paper. "Are those victim names on those papers?"

"Don't ask. Matchmaking secrets." Daisy pointed to her list again. "Once I get Carson married, I move on to Gabriel."

He cleared his throat. "As much as I'd like to see your gang settled, I thought you'd be busy planning a nursery? Picking out baby names?"

"We'll do that together. Where'd you go earlier today, anyway?"

There was no reason to tell. He didn't know exactly what he was looking for. Cosette had him worried, though. "I just checked on some things."

"You seem bothered about something."

"I'm not. I'm fine." He sat on the edge of the sofa, picked up her hand. "That's not exactly true. I'm worried about you. I wish you'd rest."

"I have plenty of time to rest."

"But this project," he said, pointing to all the materials on the table.

"Is nothing for you to concern yourself with." She blew him a kiss. "If you don't stop worrying and get close enough for me to really kiss, that's all you're going to get, I'm afraid."

That was an invitation he wasn't about to pass up. He got as close to Daisy as he could, loving the feel of her lips against his as she smooched him a good one. "I love you, Daisy. I hope you know how much."

"I love you, too."

He smiled, then realized she wasn't smiling back. "What?"

"I'm just worried that you're going to be bored here after a while. That you'll miss the lure of the open road."

"What about you? I don't imagine your motorcycle stays parked forever."

She laughed. "Have you thought about how we're going to handle getting the children around?"

He looked at her. "Side cars?"

"No." She laughed again.

"Not their own motorcycles." The thought was pretty dazzling with its own worrying consequences. He could see the next generation of Daisy's gang growing up, his sons on their own tiny motorbikes, following their mother into town. John gulped. "I can't think about that."

"I meant a van," Daisy said. "We're going to need to think about buying a van."

"Oh." He relaxed a little. "I hadn't thought that far ahead."

"We could have Dad send the limo to get us home from the hospital after the babies are born, but—"

"I'll get a van." John looked at her. "Daisy, that's a

bigger issue we need to discuss. Eventually, we have to move you out of the family compound."

"Dad owns property everywhere. We'll find something."

"No." He kissed her hand. "I mean, we'll need to move into something that *I* own."

"Would you want to own a home?"

"What do you mean?" She didn't reply, and it hit him what she was asking. "You think I'm going to pack the boys up and hit the road with them? Buy a family trailer and travel Mathison style?"

"It's not a wholly unappealing life," Daisy said.

"But not for you."

"Not for me," she said carefully. "I hope you understand."

"It's not for me, either." John hesitated. "Of course every young boy wants to rodeo, Daze."

"What if these don't?"

He shrugged. "They at least have to learn how to ride horses."

She nodded. "So we're getting our own place?"

"I think we have to."

"Is that a completely horrible thought?"

He shook his head. "Has it ever occurred to you that, of the two of us, you're much more likely to miss life on the road than I am?"

"I want you to be happy. Not stuck."

"With you, you mean." He gazed at her. "Daisy, I don't feel stuck at all. Do you?"

"Stuck? My parents were sort of stuck with each other. Strangely, I don't feel stuck. I feel like I should have swum faster in that second race and beaten Suz Hawthorne. I could have, you know."

He perked up. "Yeah. You could have. And I was a helluva prize."

"I just didn't see that like I should have."

"It's okay." He touched the Saint Michael medallion at his neck. Suddenly, he felt a sense of destiny wash over him. "Everything always works out for the best."

Even in a small town with its own mystical secrets.

Chapter Thirteen

The first chance he could get to sneak off from Daisy's watchful gaze, John headed back to the cave. He'd missed something there, he was sure of that. And Cosette's hints weren't making him feel any better about it.

His fiancée was being altogether too easygoing, even going so far as to claim she didn't mind moving out of the enormous Donovan compound. It seemed the only thing John had to do was find them their own home, and buy a van, and life would be good for him and Daisy and their children—once they convinced Cosette that she still had her hot streak. Which wasn't proving simple. But the answer supposedly was here, in this secret cavern.

He glanced around, amazed by the shiny, sparkling crystals in the walls, and the beautiful iron sconces to hold candles. There was rough seating, and even a table in the center, where Jane and Cosette had once shown him some of the BC secrets.

Jane appeared like a ghost, almost as soon as he thought about her. "Why are you here again? I thought when I rescued you here the other night, we agreed you wouldn't come down here again alone."

Her mouth turned down. "Young man, I've been

coming to this cave longer than you've been alive. I only agreed to that silly proposition of yours to make you relax. You've been quite tense lately. New fatherhood appears to be taking its toll."

"Not new fatherhood." He pondered that for a moment. "I can't get my girl to the altar. That's got me tense."

"It'll work out. I have faith in you." Jane beetled off to the table. "I might ask why *you're* here."

"I don't know why." He looked around. "Something keeps drawing me here. But it's just a cave, isn't it? And I suppose you three held your secret meetings here, you and Cosette and the sheriff, and created some kind of BC lore to keep the locals all stirred up."

Jane laughed. "Maybe. Maybe not."

Sometimes he wondered if this whole BC thing was just an elaborate gag to keep everybody in line. He wouldn't put it past the sheriff and these two ladies, and even Phillipe, to pull the town pillars routine just to keep matters serene. To keep the town in its time warp of harmony and fund-raising efforts, which the Bridesmaids Creek swim and the Best Man's Fork were: elaborate fund-raising efforts.

He sat on a rock carved out to make a nice chair, and watched Jane messing around in the box she'd pulled from the center of the table. Jane didn't look like she was in the grip of trying to orchestrate a huge ruse on the town. Her face was set in serious lines, her movements efficient. He watched her more closely, the way he'd once watched for enemy combatants.

Whatever was in that box had her complete attention.

"The town would go broke without the Bridesmaids

Creek swim and the Best Man's Fork run, wouldn't it?" he asked, suddenly struck by intuition.

"Most assuredly. Haven't you noticed how small towns are dying off in this economy? And if not the economy, then time marches on. Large land parcels get eaten up by big conglomerates. We barely dodged Robert's plans for this town. But we managed to pull the pin out of his grenade."

This grabbed his curiosity. "How did you manage that?"

Jane smiled. "Daisy, of course. We always knew she was the key to our success. You have to understand Daisy is a daddy's girl. All Robert needed was to understand how much it would mean to his daughter to have the right kind of man in her life. That man was you. And everything changed."

John wondered if he'd ever heard more malarkey in his life. "You didn't know I'd be in the picture."

"That's right. But when you came into the picture, and you were crazy about Daisy, we saw that with a little time, everything would work out for our wonderful, quaint town."

"There was no way to know that she would ever agree to marry me."

"Cosette said you were the dark horse to bet on." Jane extracted a small ledger from inside the box. She leafed through some pages. "Yes. Exactly three years ago, Cosette wrote that the man who would rescue Bridesmaids Creek had arrived."

John came to look at the ledger, peering over her shoulder. "You're not making this up. It's right there," he said, eyeing Cosette's small, neat handwriting.

"Indeed I'm not!" She glared at him. "What in the

world would make you think I'd fabricate a yarn like that?"

"I don't know. I thought you and Cosette and the sheriff, and even Phillipe, made everything up to keep people in line. Make them hop when you want them to hop."

Jane gasped. "Are you saying that you think we're fantastic storytellers? Just making this up as we go along?"

"Aren't you?"

She gave him a light whap with the ledger. "Ye of little faith. You're sitting in a secret cave that we've allowed no one else to learn of, and you have to ask?"

"You let me into the club because I'm the—"

"Yes, yes," Jane said impatiently, "you're the man who's going to save Bridesmaids Creek."

He liked the sound of that, especially if it meant he'd finally get Daisy to an altar, but something was off in the story. "Save it from what, exactly?"

Her eyes went wide. "Why, save it from itself, of course. Extinction."

"I thought Robert Donovan was the enemy, once upon a time."

"Does he act like an enemy now?"

"No. He'd like to help as much as anyone."

"All right, then. Now you know."

He wasn't sure what he knew. "I know that BC is a wonderful place to raise a family."

"Yes." She put the ledger back in its box and slid it into the table. "What else do you know, Einstein?"

He looked into her eyes. "That you're handing the wands over to Daisy and me. That we, and our friends you've recently dispatched to the altar, are the future."

"Now you're getting somewhere."

That was the key. The town had to stay young, in order to grow. Stay vibrant. Daisy and he would take over important roles, and their children would grow up steeped in the lore. "But how do I get her to finally say I do? She's all worried about Cosette getting her magic back. So worried she won't get married until Cosette feels like she's had a hand in running it."

"Do you expect Daisy not to want the magic for herself?" Jane looked at him steadily.

"No. She wants everything BC that every other bride has had."

"Can you blame her?"

He shook his head.

"Then my suggestion is you give her that very thing. And then you'll have Daisy Donovan, and everything will be all right."

Jane marched to the front of the cave. He followed, thinking to walk her to her vehicle, but she was nowhere to be seen. She'd just vanished, like some kind of spirit.

A delicate spirit with plenty of sass.

He thought for a moment, then walked back inside the cave and pulled out the ledger to look at it for himself.

It is early morning here in Bridesmaids Creek. There isn't much but dusty, barren fields. We rode here by wagon, and my family back home said they can't see why we'd choose this place to settle.
—Eliza Chatham

John flipped to the front of the ledger to look at the hand-drawn family tree. Eliza Chatham's name was at the top, the first resident of Bridesmaids Creek, and Jane's great-great-great-grandmother. John saw that there had been a Hiram Chatham, but whatever had happened to him had been rubbed out. Or had faded. Hiram wasn't on the same line with Eliza; she was accorded the top spot. Beside her name was written Founder of Bridesmaids Creek.

John flipped through some deeds that had been filed, all in Eliza's name. There were pages and pages of notations, each filled out in neat handwriting. He took the ledger over to the light to settle in for a good read. Then the ledger shut tight, snapping closed with a click. He tried to open it again, but it was sealed, somehow stuck fast.

He went back to the table, to the seat where Jane had been sitting, taking the closed ledger with him. It stayed clam-like and stubborn, and though John would have once thought that was impossible, now he knew that Bridesmaids Creek simply wasn't ready to give up all its secrets to an outsider.

Not yet. He wasn't one of them, even if he'd been handpicked to become an unmatchmaker, whatever that was. A newer version of dusty, history-loving Phillipe.

Maybe he wasn't cut out for this type of steadfast responsibility. Taking on this role would mean he'd be forever tied to one place, a keeper of a town flame.

The worry passed as fast as it had come, extinguished by the sudden vision of Daisy and his future children that popped into his head. He smiled, loving the picture. Maybe Daisy was right: maybe he hadn't seen himself spending his life exactly tied to one location, one way of life.

But he could see himself bound to Daisy, and the binding would feel wonderful every day of his life.

First he had to get the magic to accept him. Allow him to take Phillipe's place.

"No doubt the only way to do that is to marry Daisy, since this is a wedding-happy town."

The ledger stayed locked in his hands, resisting him. John realized he'd been expecting it to fall open, once he uttered the magic verbal key. There was something else he was missing, but whatever that was, it seemed determined to elude him.

Daisy was eluding him, too.

He put the ledger securely back into its hiding place and went to find the most beautiful, motorcycle-riding mother of his children a man could ever hope to have.

And he did hope to have her. Soon.

IF THERE WAS something magic about Bridesmaids Creek, it appeared that John wasn't going to experience it. He spent the next two months assisting the town with rebuilding the jail, and helping put Cosette's shop— actually Daisy's gang's dating-service cigar-bar thing— back together, and still John didn't have the epiphany he knew he needed. Daisy was much bigger now, staying very still when he was around, though he knew that was largely for his benefit. When he wasn't with her, he could guess that she kept the mansion pretty active, like a beehive. She hadn't changed a bit from the woman he'd chased up to Montana, and that was one of the things he loved most about her.

She had her gang coming by, and Cosette, and sometimes the sheriff. Cosette had found time to knit baby booties, three pairs of blue ones that were so small they could probably only fit on a doll. Reality smacked John in the face as he realized his boys were going to start out very tiny, and he went a bit weak in the knees.

He went home to see Daisy, tell her that magic or no, it was time.

"Marry me," he said as she lay on the sofa.

She smiled at him. "I thought you'd never ask."

He stopped. "Just like that?"

"Of course just like that. If you've finally made up your mind—"

"Hey!" He went to sit next to her, looking at the burgeoning mound that was his fiancée's stomach. "My mind has been made up for years. *Years.*"

They sat together for a few minutes, and he stroked her hair. "How are you feeling?"

"The nurse came by today to check my contractions. Tomorrow I go on some kind of drip."

He sat straight up. "Is there a problem?"

"No. Not really. The drip will help the babies stay inside a little while longer. Longer is better."

He took that under advisement. "I guess you shouldn't have a whole lot of excitement."

She giggled. "What did you have in mind? Dad and Barclay are out looking over a property, and I could—"

Her small hand stroked dangerously close, an obvious invitation to please him. John picked up her hand, kissed it. "I don't think I can concentrate."

"I bet I could get you to concentrate," she teased.

He felt like a thousand wires were short-circuiting his brain. "Daisy, I could be a father any day now. You and I could be parents. Literally any second."

"Does that scare you?"

"Hell, yes!" He thought about that for a second. "And no. But mostly yes. There's so much to do!"

"And speaking of doing things, you'll never guess what I've got scheduled for next week." Daisy looked proud of herself. "You are looking at a woman who has the first phase of matchmaking apprenticeship well in hand." She took a deep breath. "I've set up a Bridesmaids Creek swim for next week!"

"Wait a minute, Daze," John began, then reminded himself he needed to be supportive. This was a big step for her. Besides which, their marriage would start off on a good footing if Daisy felt that she had made up for past transgressions in BC. "I mean, that's great, babe. Really awesome. It's not too much excitement for you? Considering the IV you're getting tomorrow?"

"Well, obviously I didn't know about the IV when I set this up. But it's going to be fabulous!" She pretty much glowed as she sat up, getting more excited as she relayed her big news. "I've got all *five* of my gang swimming!"

"Swimming for brides?" He wondered if any of Daisy's gang had truly given up the idea of catching her for themselves.

"I have wonderful local girls participating. There was more interest than I thought there'd be."

"You didn't expect your gang to be a draw for the ladies?"

She smiled at him. "I wasn't sure. They haven't done a whole lot of dating over the years."

He kissed her hand, enjoying the closeness. "But you think that now you're off the market, they may be more open to looking around for wives."

She nodded. "And the local beauties are definitely excited!"

Nothing could go wrong with this plan, could it? He had a funny feeling there was a hook in here somewhere, a hook with his name on it. "So, back to our own special vows, Daisy."

"Yes?" She smiled, and he took a deep breath.

"How about if I give Sam a shout to come over and do his thing?"

Her expression turned serious. "It's so sudden."

"Tomorrow you'll have an IV," he reminded her.

"That's true." She swallowed hard. "I don't have a veil. Or anything."

"We could have a more elaborate wedding ceremony in the summer."

"True." She carefully considered that, nodding. "All right. See if Sam can come over."

Her face caught his attention, stopping him in mid-dial. "You don't want to do this, do you?"

"No, it's fine." Daisy nodded. "I'm ready, I really am."

She didn't sound ready. In fact, she might have sounded reluctant.

Of course it was no woman's idea of a big day. But he had to get her to say *I do*, before his babies were born.

He'd fix everything else later.

Chapter Fourteen

Daisy and John were married the day before the big race was set to happen. John could tell his bride was nervous about the huge event she'd organized—more nervous than getting married, more nervous than the nurse coming to give her the new medication.

But they were married now, thanks to Sam, with Barclay as a witness, and Robert giving his daughter away. John felt he was the luckiest man in the world.

"Thank you," he told Daisy, because that was the first thing that popped out of his mouth, and because it was truly how he felt now that she was his bride. *Grateful* was the first word that came to mind, as well as *relieved*.

She smiled. "Thank you?"

"Yes, thank you very much, Mrs. Mathison, for becoming my wife and making me the happiest man on the planet."

"I still say you could have done better," Sam said woefully to Daisy, "like me."

They all laughed because the last person to ever say *I do* would be Sam Barr. Sam was many things but a marrying man wasn't one of them.

"Welcome to the family, son," Robert said, shaking

John's hand. "For a wedding gift, I hope you'll accept half ownership of this house, and an office building in Australia."

John coughed, finding himself suddenly out of breath.

"Thank you, Daddy," Daisy said, hugging her father from her perch on the sofa.

John couldn't believe what he was hearing. "Hang on a second, Daze, babe," he began, but Sam grabbed his arm, steering him toward the punch bowl Barclay had set up in the den.

"Careful, buddy," Sam said, his voice low. "I know you've been caught off guard, but you'll want to take a few deep breaths in order to start your married life off on the right foot."

John felt as if all the air was being sucked out of him. "I don't want half this house, or a building in Australia!"

"Easy, hoss." Sam pulled out a flask and dumped a bit of extra party fun into the glass of punch he handed to John. "It's not about what you want, it's about what Daisy expects and what she knows is to be hers. Don't get in the middle of family wrangling, is my advice. You're family now, but Daisy and Ty are Robert's flesh and blood. He's going to do for them what he wants to, and you'll sound ungrateful if you try to back out now. It's Daisy's share, if you see what I'm saying."

"I can take care of my own wife!"

"I know you can," Sam soothed. "But you knew what you were marrying into, buddy. This isn't a woman who grew up in a trailer following the rodeo circuit."

John tried to follow Sam's rationale through the crazy, panicked haze enveloping him. "I don't want any of that stuff."

"You might not, but she will. Take my advice, zip your lips, dude. Smile and say thank-you."

"He's going to think I married his daughter for money! He all but accused me of it in the beginning!"

"Words spoken in haste continue to live on," Sam said sternly. "Listen to your pastoral counsel, because it's all you've got at the moment."

"Helluva pastor you are," John grumbled. He swigged some more punch, delighted to see Cosette and Jane rush into the room for the small wedding party they'd planned for after the vows. They handed Daisy gifts and hugged her, and made a big deal out of her, as if she truly was the revered daughter of the town she'd always wanted to be.

He felt a warm glow start inside him. It was all going to work out. The Bridesmaids Creek charm had been wrong: he had found a bride, and he had married her in Bridesmaids Creek, and it was great.

Phillipe and Sheriff McAdams came in, followed by Daisy's gang. John didn't think he'd ever get past calling them *the meatheads* in his own mind. They greeted him, disappointment etched pretty deeply in their faces.

Still, they were trying to man up. John nodded at them. "Thanks for the congratulations. I know I'm a lucky guy."

"The best girl in Bridesmaids Creek," Carson said, "and you got her."

"I know," John said, "I realize how fortunate I am."

"Some might say it was just luck," Red said.

John laughed. "I don't think so."

"Could have been." Gabriel shrugged. "Not that we're not happy for you."

But they weren't jumping up and down like excited

Christmas elves. "It's all right. I get it. You guys have known her all her life. She's special. Trust me, I'll take great care of Daisy."

In fact he couldn't wait to do just that. Sometimes it was hard to believe that she was having his sons—three sons!—and now she was actually his.

"It'll never stick," Dig said.

John's happy thoughts did a nosedive. "It's going to stick. Let me get you guys a beer. You're awfully hot under the collars."

Their beefy lunkheads looked like they might be about to start smoking. John realized the whole room was staring at him and the gang, listening intently.

"Barclay," John said, "I think these guys may need a beer. Or six," he said under his breath. "Maybe with a sleeping potion in it."

Barclay went to retrieve the beer, and John went back to join the gang. It was time to make nice.

Daisy deserved this, at least.

"So we hear you're now the owner of half this place," Carson said, glancing around.

"And commercial real estate in Australia," Red said.

John wanted terribly to refute that. It sounded awful, the way they'd said it, as if he was some kind of gold-digging cowboy. And that was the way they meant it. He hadn't won Daisy in a Bridesmaids Creek swim, the way things were done here, and yet he'd fallen into a fortune.

"Sitting in pretty tall cotton, I'd say, for a Navy SEAL who just works a farm," Gabriel said.

"I'm not a part owner—" John began.

"Yes, that was very generous of Robert," Sam inserted smoothly, coming to join them. "Completely unexpected gesture, but Robert has shown his generosity to the town quite a bit lately."

There was no arguing with that. Daisy's gang stood around for a moment like floor ornaments, and John decided it was now time to make his escape. "My bride—"

"Thing is," Dig said, "it's a shame the best girl in the town didn't get what she deserved."

"Ah, well," Clint said. "We'll all be in our own races tomorrow. Daisy's brought in some great gals for us, though she won't tell us who. It's going to be a total adventure."

John wondered if one could poke a guest in the nose at their own wedding party. Several noses, in fact, distinctly needed a poking.

"I never did quite understand how a Navy SEAL could come up with a leg cramp." Carson's face wore an expression of confusion. "Isn't that what SEALs do? Swim? Stay in shape?"

"Swim, as they say, like a SEAL?" Red gibed, turning up the torture on John a notch.

"Listen—" John began.

"He swims fine, fellows," Sam said. "Lay off the guy, huh? It's his big night. He'll never get married again."

"No, but he'll probably get divorced," Red said, sounding happy about the possibility. "You'll see."

"That's silly. I don't believe in juju and the tales from the crypt you people spin around here," John said, overriding Sam, who was trying to shush him.

"Tales from the crypt might be a bit harsh," Sam said. "Come on, buddy, let's get you some wedding cake."

"We don't have any wedding cake." John stopped, catching sight of Daisy. She was staring at him, her eyes huge. Belatedly he realized she'd overheard everything—

as had everyone else in the room. Suz and Mackenzie Hawthorne had come in while he wasn't paying attention, along with their husbands Cisco and Justin. Jade and Ty Spurlock had arrived, and Jade's mother, Betty. Everyone had witnessed his unfortunate remark. It also came to him that Daisy had no veil, and no bouquet. She'd simply worn a white caftan as her wedding gown.

He gulped. At least he'd gotten her a ring, although her hands were so swollen she'd put the ring on her pinky and said it would be lovely when it fit, after she had the babies and maybe a few months after that.

Maybe the meatheads were right. A horrible gnawing sensation settled into his stomach. What if Daisy woke up one day and realized their relationship was totally uneven? That he'd never be able to provide her with real estate around the world, that he would never be wealthy like her father. He could certainly afford a house in town, and it wouldn't be one on wheels, but it would definitely require a thirty-year mortgage.

"Don't let them get to you!" Sam said. "Come on, let's get you a congratulatory cigar. Outside. Where we can get some good, bracing fresh air into you."

"I don't want a cigar." He watched Daisy as she chatted with their friends, enjoying her big moment.

But it wasn't the big moment of which she'd dreamed.

"I can hear you thinking, buddy. You need to let it all go." Sam dragged him to a corner, poured a little more whiskey into his glass. "Listen, you and Daisy share equal blame here. She avoided you winning her."

Perhaps that was true, and Sam had his back for saying so, but it didn't matter. "I just don't want Daisy to have any regrets."

"She'll regret you standing around looking like you've

lost your best friend if you don't pull up. Get a grip on yourself, man! Don't let those dumb asses rile you. They're trying to. Don't let them win."

He was already riled. In fact, he was worried.

"So it's a swim tomorrow, is it?" John asked Daisy's ex-gang.

"It is," Clint said. "Lots of ladies to be won, I hear."

"Not that you'd know what to do with one if you caught her," John said, "but I think I'll join you fellows."

"Join us?" Gabriel asked, and the five men perked up, staring at him with sudden interest.

"Buddy, slow down a bit, think what you're doing here," Sam said, low, the way they used to talk to each other in dangerous locations. Low and encouraging— and warning.

"Yeah. I think I'll join you." John drew himself up. "I think I'll win Daisy all over again."

"No!" Daisy exclaimed, her voice in a chorus with Sheriff McAdams's, Cosette's and Jane's.

"No?" John looked at them. "I want to win my wife, fair and square."

"No, John—" Daisy began, but Dig grabbed his hand, shaking it.

"We'll save a spot for you," Dig said. "Right up at the starting splash."

"Yeah. See if you can live down that leg cramp problem, okay?" Red asked.

"The only cramping there'll be tomorrow is a cramp in your miniscule brains when you realize that I've outswum you by a mile."

No one in the room was smiling, except for Daisy's gang, and they looked like their typical jack-o'-lantern-headed selves.

"Can I see you outside a moment, buddy?" Sam

dragged him away and gestured him to follow him several yards from the house, where no one could overhear. "Dude, what the hell are you doing?"

"Showing my wife that we were always meant to be together. Nothing's ever going to separate us. There's no BC charm that I wouldn't buy into to win Daisy. No weird BC backfire's going to…backfire on us."

"That's what you don't get. It's a trap, John."

"A trap?"

"Yes! And you walked right into it." Sam looked despondent. "You dummy. Why do you always leap before you look?"

"Me?" John laughed. "I think that's your calling card, Sam. Leaping before looking."

"No, I'm a strategist and you're a grab-the-ring guy." Sam sighed. "You realize that if you don't win tomorrow, you make everything worse?"

"How?"

"Because everyone in this town knows that the races are all-important. Daisy isn't supposed to get another one. Three's the charm."

"Says who?" John growled.

"Says the legend."

Sam seemed pretty adamant. A little more worry crept into John. "I've lived all across the USA and there was never any town as lost in its mind games as this one. You have to admit that, Sam."

"It's too late to back out and claim you don't believe."

"Why? What will happen if I lose?"

Sam took a deep breath. "You lose Daisy. Maybe not tomorrow, maybe not the next day, but eventually."

"Bull." He loved Daisy. They were meant to be together. No goofy town crystal ball wackiness was going to change that.

"It will happen, because she'll know," Sam warned. "It's not juju, it's who Daisy is. She's a daughter of Bridesmaids Creek. And she *believes*. Think, John, all her life she's seen the magic work. She believes it, wants it desperately for herself. But she's not going to get it. And you weren't even supposed to have a marriage in BC, Cosette said so. You blew it. Only somehow, because you're crazy, I guess, you figured out a way to make it happen, anyway."

"No, I didn't," John said slowly, realization dawning on him. "*You* did."

Sam was silently watching him. A chill crept over John's scalp. The thing about Sam that very few people knew was that, beneath the banter, beneath the fun and games, Sam was a helluva thinker. He was Mensa-gifted, with a brain that was always working, two gears ahead of the next guy. They'd relied on him for those gears—Ty and Cisco and John were probably alive because of Sam and his ways.

"You got yourself certified to perform weddings because you knew something would keep getting in the way for Daisy and me here in Bridesmaids Creek. So you decided to perform it outside of BC, with an online class or something that would vest you with the power. You went around BC, in effect. You countermanded the charm," John said.

"I figured it might be something like getting married at sea. You know how if you're so many miles out, you're bound by different laws than when you're on solid ground?" Sam nodded with satisfaction. "That's what I did. I decided to perform your wedding with powers vested in me that were not of the solid ground of BC."

"That's a helluva thing to do for a friend."

"A fellow SEAL," Sam said. "You'd have done it for me. So don't go blowing it now. I've put a lot of effort into this plan. I don't need you lighting it on fire."

"I have to do the race." John knew this as sure as he knew his name was John Lopez Mathison. "The only way I'll ever really have Daisy's heart is to win it. The same way the other brides in this town were won." He thought about the cave and the ledger, knew how long and deep the traditions were here. "The charms are important, more important than I ever realized."

"All right, then. Now that you know that truth, that's half the battle." Sam snapped his fingers. "All you have to do now is march yourself inside, tell them you took leave of your senses, and that there's no way in hell you're going to horn in on the big day that Daisy planned and worked so hard on."

Easier said than done.

Chapter Fifteen

"What?" John stared at Sam. "I'm not going to do that!"

"You have no idea how hard Daisy has worked on her conversion. Her rebirth in this town," Sam said sternly. "Don't be selfish, dude."

"Selfish?" John was agog. "I'm trying to give her her big day!"

"*Tomorrow* is her big day. She planned it, she set it in motion. She's taking on the crown of Madame Matchmaker. This isn't about you. This is about *her*."

There was some twisted logic going on, and John wasn't sure what his buddy was trying to do to him. Taking a deep breath, he reminded himself that Sam always, always had another level in his game, sometimes just to watch people spin themselves into knots.

"I'm not going to be talked out of this," John said quietly.

"That's your pride talking. You only want to race because those five troublemakers razzed you about it. You're still embarrassed about that cramp. Let it go, is my advice."

He couldn't. He couldn't let Daisy go. Sure, he had her—they were married—but every woman deserved to have her heart won. Every man wanted to know that his woman's heart belonged to him totally until the end of time. And Daisy was a daughter of Bridesmaids Creek. The magic that flowed here—or even if it was just superstition—flowed in her, too.

He thought about the ledger sealing itself shut when he'd tried to read further. Despite Cosette and Jane letting him into the secrets of BC, BC itself hadn't yet accepted him as one of its own. He had to win Bridesmaids Creek's daughter's heart—Daisy's—if he ever truly wanted to belong in Bridesmaids Creek, so that Daisy would know he'd given every last inch of everything he had to win her.

That was how fairy tales worked.

"What is this, a secret SEAL gathering?" Cosette and Jane appeared in their midst. "If you're done saying your piece, Sam, I'll take a turn at fricasseeing him."

"I'm not sure anything I'm saying is getting through his thick skull."

"It is thicker than normal," Jane observed. "John, what are you thinking?" She held up a hand. "Never mind. I know what you're thinking. You're outrunning ghosts."

"It's not possible to outrun ghosts, Jane, if there were such a thing as ghosts." John regretted that statement the moment it came out of his mouth. Both the women gasped and Sam shook his head at him.

"I mean, I know there are ghosts and spirits and things," he said, trying to dig himself out. "What I'm trying to say is that this isn't a ghost issue."

"Because you're not trying to outrun yours or anything." Cosette stood on tiptoe to peer into his eyes for a second, then settled back on her feet.

"Were you trying to look into my soul?" John demanded.

"I was checking to see if the secret sauce Sam's been pouring you is addling your brain," Cosette shot back.

"For someone who doesn't think they're affected by ghosts, you sure do seem antsy," Sam observed. "Good grief."

John sighed. "If you came out here to talk me out of competing tomorrow, you're wasting your time and might as well be back inside eating cake."

"You didn't buy any wedding cake," Jane observed. "Lucky for you, I brought a beauty. Betty Harper and Cosette helped me with it, and it's my finest masterpiece. In fact, Daisy told us to tell you to get a move on and help her cut it. She wants to stuff some cake into your face—er, your piehole."

"She's unhappy with me," John said.

"What do you think? You're horning in on her big day," Sam said, scoffing. "It's supposed to be about her, her big moment the only way she can have it. You're turning it into a day that's all about you."

"Nuts," John said. "When you say it like that, I actually hear the voice of reason. Lucky for you, I'm pretty deaf."

"So stubborn," Cosette whispered to Jane, loud enough for John to hear. "Listen, as head matchmaker in this one-stoplight town—"

"Two. I think we're getting another one," Jane said, "although one never knows how these rumors get started."

"As head matchmaker," Cosette continued, "I'm going to make an educated guess and tell you that you're only doing this because Robert's generous gift freaked you out."

"I don't want his money," John said. "Put your mind at ease on that. I'm well aware that he's doing everything for Daisy."

"You don't have to deserve it," Jane said, "or live up to Robert's success in any way."

"Not that you could," Sam said helpfully. "It makes me laugh just to imagine you living in this heap."

Daisy's home was hardly a heap. John wondered if his friends were deliberately trying to bounce on his nerves and get a rise out of him. "I'm not trying to prove myself to anyone. Except Daisy. Which is why I'm participating tomorrow, and nothing you can say will change my mind. But thanks for caring." He hugged the ladies, gave Sam a swat on the shoulder. "I'm off to help my bride cut the cake."

"Be careful," Sam called after him. "Daisy's got great aim."

She did at that. John grinned, and walked faster. If his bride wanted to feed him cake from her dainty fingertips, he couldn't get there soon enough.

And tomorrow, after he'd won her by all measurements that mattered in Bridesmaids Creek, she was going to experience the magic she'd always wanted.

He understood about needing to fit in. He really did.

"John," Daisy said that night when he crawled up next to her on a divan he aligned by her chaise, "I'm going to give you some sleeping pills tonight so you can't race tomorrow."

He laughed, wrapped his arms carefully around her. She was big as a moose, and felt like it, too, but somehow, John always made her feel delicate, desirable. "Even sleeping pills wouldn't keep me from my goal, gorgeous."

She rolled to look at him, moving like a floundering hippopotamus. "I don't want you to do this."

He seemed to decide he was more interested in her lips than in what they were saying. The kisses he suddenly stroked across her mouth made her brain scatter its thoughts.

"John!" She gave him a tiny push backward so she could gaze up into his eyes, even though all she really wanted was him kissing her. But this was important. "Don't let my gang goad you into this."

"I should have done it a long time ago." He picked up her hand, kissing it as if she was some kind of princess. He made her feel like a princess. "You deserve all the magic in the world, Daze."

Her breath caught. "You know I love you, don't you?"

"Yes, I do." He grinned. "How could you not love a rascal like me?"

"I do love you, and you don't have to win me. Or whatever it is you think you're doing tomorrow."

"I'm winning you. There's no thinking about it." John gazed down at her with eyes that said he found her very sexy. "And, Mrs. Mathison, you're going to like being won."

Her breath caught again, and Daisy told herself to breathe, to tell John why him going on the creek swim was such a bad idea. He didn't understand the ways of BC.

But it was oh, so tempting. What woman didn't want to be won by a handsome, god-bodied hunk of a man? "The thing is, I'm already yours."

"That's bothering me a bit. I'm not sure I trust Sam's certificate of authenticity."

"What do you mean?"

"He says he got this online power of marriage thingy, but it's Sam we're talking about. Do we know for sure?"

Daisy hesitated. "That's a terrible thing to say about your brother. He wouldn't let us go around thinking we were legally married. I'm having children soon. He'll be a godfather." She looked at him, ran a hand over his strong chest. "Go back to kissing me. You need to get your mind off of crazy stuff."

"It's not crazy if we're talking about Sam."

"Okay, well, then, this need you have to justify your racing tomorrow…" She looked up at him, stroked his lip with her finger. "I don't care about that stupid leg cramp."

He caught her hands in his. "You don't think I can win, do you, buttercup?"

"I'm telling you that I don't care if you do."

"Oh, you care. This is Bridesmaids Creek, so you most definitely care. Besides which, women with fathers who pass out real estate in dream locations think highly of themselves. They want to be won." He kissed her nose. "In your case, you deserve to be wooed and won." He worked his way from the tip of her nose to her lips, giving her a kiss that made her heart race. "Besides which, beautiful, you can't tell me BC doesn't care about this. Jane and Cosette said that once word got out that the SEAL who cramped up before was having another shot at it, ticket sales went crazy."

Daisy sighed. Pulled back a little. "This is all about your ego."

"No, this is about my beautiful wife." He kissed her

shoulder, and Daisy fought the urge to wriggle closer to his wonderfully roving mouth. "I want you, Daisy Donovan Mathison. I intend to have you forever."

He certainly didn't seem to notice that her belly was shaped like three basketballs were rolling around inside her. "It will all be nothing," she said airily. "I won't be there to see."

"You're not supposed to leave this bed, anyway. Unless I carry you out into the garden room." He kissed her again, stealing her breath.

"Oh, John, would you mind? Could you?"

He laughed. "Of course I can. You're light as a feather."

She was not light as a feather, unless the feather was glued to a two hundred pound weight. "You're trying to romance me into giving in. But I really don't want you to compete against my guys."

He carefully picked her up, carried her to the garden room she loved so much. "Their tiny little egos will still be fine after I spank them soundly. I have no idea what women you'd find to be the prizes, but I'm sure you found some real honeys."

Daisy looked out the window, marveling at each change in the fall-blooming landscape. "It's so beautiful. This is my favorite room in the house."

"I know. If you look out in the garden near that awesome statue of the naked lady—"

"John," Daisy said, laughing.

"Can you see it?"

She leaned forward, peering outside eagerly. "I don't see anything."

"That's right. Because there's nothing there. Yet." He grinned, and her heart did a funny little flip.

"Yet?"

"That's right." He pulled out a long white scroll with a gold bow wrapped around it, handing it to her with a flourish. "But there will be something in the garden very soon, if you accept my wedding gift."

"Do I unwrap this?" She could hardly wait to see what he was up to.

"Go. Just remember it's only a gift, it's not set in stone. It's something I'm hoping we can do together."

"I can't wait to see." She ripped off the bow and unwrapped the scroll. "Oh, John! A waterfall!"

He leaned close. "Obviously these are just some initial plans. Your father thought we might take out the statue out there, despite her lovely nakedness, and put the waterfall there." He grinned, pleased with his surprise. "You see I stayed within the keeping of the Bridesmaids Creek theme with the water element. And I thought we could christen the waterfall with some creek water for the effects only Bridesmaids Creek seems to have."

She laughed. "I love it. Thank you so much. It's a wonderful wedding gift."

He kissed her. "You're the wonderful wedding gift, Daisy. I waited a long time to have you, and it was definitely worth the wait."

"So you're okay with Dad's present?" She looked at him, trying to read his expression.

"At first I was startled. Any man would be," he said. "But then I realized I didn't care what came with the package, because all I wanted was the package, anyway." He kissed her shoulder again, just the way she longed for him to do.

She smiled. "I'm the happiest woman on the planet. I really believe I am."

"Good." He stood. "I have to carry you back into the other room now. I was under strict orders from your nurse to bring you in here, give you your gift and get you back to your command center."

"Oh." Her face fell a bit. She glanced back toward the beautiful garden. She'd missed getting to see this during the time she'd been bed bound. "Thank you, John. It means so much to me that you brought me out here."

"I know, babe." He scooped her up as if she was no heavier than a bag of marshmallows. "You like looking at that naked lady out there, don't lie."

She laughed. "That naked lady happens to be a lovely rendering of the goddess Diana."

"I'd rather have a lovely rendering of you in my garden, but then I'd never get any work done." He laid her carefully on the sofa bed again. "However, I get to have you in my bed every night, so that's even better."

She smiled up at him. "Me and three little babies very soon."

"Not too soon. Let's not be jumping the gun, little lady. Whew, one of us needs to bulk up a bit." He flexed the muscles in his arms, winking. "These big strong guns you see before you are going to get me to the finish line tomorrow way ahead of the other combatants."

"John," Daisy said, "sit down here a moment."

He sat next to her. "One day, babe, you're going to invite me to your bed for a whole other reason besides idle chitchat."

"This isn't idle chitchat." She tried not to think about how much she'd enjoyed the many times she'd been in a bed, or anywhere for that matter, with John. "This is absolutely serious. You can't race tomorrow."

"Don't you worry, beautiful." He leaned back against

the sofa, his grin confident. "You're going to have your big day."

Daisy took a deep breath. "It already is my big day, because I set everything up. Not to underappreciate what you're trying to do for me—it's very sweet and romantic—but you really shouldn't. And saying that Sam probably didn't legally marry us is just you trying too hard to give me what you think I want. What I want I already have." She put a hand on her stomach. "I have you, and my babies. What else is there? That's magic enough for me, darling."

He put his hand over hers as it rested on her belly. "Once the babies are born, I want a wedding where you and I are married in front of our friends, your father gives you away, and my family rolls into town to throw birdseed at us."

Who would have ever thought John would be such a traditional guy? She loved him all the more for it. "Even if you win tomorrow—"

"*When* I win tomorrow."

"Nothing changes, John," she continued, desperate to make him see. "You and I are already married."

"Yeah, but Cisco raced for Suz after they were already married. You have to admit that was well-played. Did wonders for their marriage."

Suz and Cisco were two of the happiest people she knew. "But it's different this time. If you don't win, everyone will always question whether we were meant to be."

"I won't. I know we are."

She had to love a man who had so much confidence it seemed to rub off on her, too. Daisy reminded herself to keep to her mission, and not focus on his long, lean body. "John, as a matchmaker's apprentice, my reputation as a matchmaker must be absolute."

"Meaning?"

She thought his eyelids were starting to drift lower now that he'd gotten comfy on her bed. His hunky body had relaxed into languid, sexy lines that had her gulping a little. "Meaning that if you don't win, I'll look like a matchmaker who can't handle her own match. You saw what's happened to Cosette and Phillipe now that they've gotten divorced."

His eyes popped open. "The ol' magic wand emptied out?"

She nodded.

"Still swimming, Daze. The way I see it, when I win, your magic will be red-hot. Blazing. That wand of yours will be shooting sparks. The ladies and fellows will come from miles around to get a dose of your spellbound ways."

He wasn't listening. He wasn't going to change his mind. It was maddening, but it was also quite endearing. Daisy felt herself fall just a little bit more in love with her husband. "You could actually undo our magic if you don't win," she said, finally stating the real reason he absolutely couldn't race.

"No, I won't. Cisco didn't." He sat up. "In fact, Suz didn't even tell Cisco he shouldn't race for her."

"Because they were keeping their marriage a secret. From me. From everyone. Cisco had to race."

"Didn't matter, doll face. They're perfectly happy."

"Because Cisco won."

"And I'm going to win."

She looked at him, and he looked at her, and the seconds stretched by.

"You don't think I can."

She smiled. "We've had three chances. None of them really panned out."

"So? It's just a race. Just a fund-raiser."

"There's no such thing as 'just' anything in BC. Which you should know by now." Daisy took a deep breath. "The thing is, if you don't win, John, I'll never have any magic at all."

"Why? What does that mean?"

"It means that no one tempts BC's charms. I don't have more than three chances at the magic. No one gets a fourth, it just doesn't work that way."

"There you have it. No one gets a fourth, no one's ever tried. It'll be fine, because all that legend crap is just a bunch of hokum, anyway."

He didn't look as if he quite believed what he was saying. Daisy knew that John was plenty aware of the enchanted ways of Bridesmaids Creek; he was just being stubborn as an ornery old mule. "We don't do hokum in BC. It's all very well established, and the magic is recorded in a ledger somewhere. Cosette and Jane keep records of all these things. It's quite serious."

"I know," he grumbled. "I'm an outsider. I come from a family of people who don't believe in magic. I'm the most superstitious person in my family, and they think I'm a little weird about it. My mother does cowboy preaching. She never thinks about anything to do with enchantment." He took a deep breath. "The only thing my family believes in is hard work. It doesn't earn us much money, we don't own office buildings in faraway lands and we don't have a mansion. Our house rolls on wheels 365 days a year, even birthdays and Christmas. My brothers and I were all born in different towns. What I'm trying to say, Daze, is that I've got my reasons for competing tomorrow, and I'm comfortable with that."

Chapter Sixteen

"He's so pigheaded he's impossible," Daisy told her father the next day when he came in to visit. Her IV had been inserted, and she was lying here, trying to be still, when all she really wanted to do was hop out of bed and ride her motorcycle to the creek to see what was happening on the biggest day of her newly formed magic wand.

"I think you like that about John," Robert said with a grin. "He's quite won me over with his determination to pursue you."

"He doesn't need to pursue me. We're married." Daisy shook her head. "I'm surrounded by lovingly obtuse, romantic-to-their-core males who can't see the big picture for the trees!"

"It's not altogether a bad thing." Robert seemed quite tickled to be lumped in with his son-in-law. "You know, life seems awfully good from where I'm sitting. I've got a new son-in-law, a new daughter-in-law, a son I didn't know I had and a bunch of grandbabies. I say if the man wants to run or race or fly a kite, let him take a crack at it."

"If he doesn't win this time, it's going to be disastrous."

"Life's about chances," Robert said philosophically.

Why was she talking about this to her father? He of all people believed in rolling the dice, taking big risks. "Dad, John isn't like us. He's sensitive. He doesn't take things in stride."

"Some would say we've come a long way ourselves."

"Yes, but deep inside, I always knew I was going to be all right. We had to work harder to be together, so we'd appreciate it more. So when John got that leg cramp and came in last that day, it was actually the magic on our side. He can't go and mess it up now by losing again!"

"Who says he will?"

"Have you seen my gang lately? They're ripped like ridges on a mountain. This is their big moment, their chance at the brass ring. All the new guys to town are out of the game. Justin, John, Cisco and even Ty himself are matched up and married."

"Not Sam."

"Sam doesn't count. He won't race. The only time he ever even threatened to race was just to get his buddies goosed up to the starting line." Daisy laughed. "Sam isn't the marrying kind."

"It's a rare man who isn't."

Daisy looked at her father. "Of course there's you. You're not married."

He held up a hand. "Yes, but I have been, and I'm not looking to do it at my age. In fact, now that I've given this house to you and Ty, I think I'm going to move."

Daisy gasped. "Why?"

"Because you lovebirds need your own nest. Besides," Robert said, getting all excited, "I think I'll buy that ghost house."

"Dad! Not the abandoned Martin place! Those love-struck bank robbers lived there and ran cattle, but couldn't turn a profit. Why would you want to do that?" Daisy couldn't imagine anyplace she'd rather live less, and she sure didn't want her father out there. "It's been empty forever, Dad. It's going to have all kinds of rats and roaches and things. You'll stay here with us."

"Don't forget the ghosts. I'm really looking forward to those." Robert rubbed his hands gleefully. "Of course you know there's no such things as ghosts. Those bank robbers aren't still hanging around in paranormal form."

"Dad, there's no reason for you to leave."

"There can only be one king in a castle. This place belongs to your brother and you now. And your families." He looked pleased. "For an old man, I'd say I've done pretty well. I'm looking forward to a new project."

"If you're looking for a new project, start Betty Harper up in a business selling her Christmas cookies. They're works of art. Or get my guys out of the space where Cosette and Phillipe belong. We don't need a cigar bar in this town." Daisy sat up a little. "That space belongs to Cosette and Phillipe, anyway."

"I don't know," Robert said. "The guys like that location pretty well. They claim they're getting all kinds of calls."

"For cigars, and hookers."

"Hookers?" Robert raised a brow. "That doesn't sound right."

"Well, how many men go to a cigar bar looking for a bride? None that I know of."

"You have a point. We certainly can't get that kind of reputation in BC."

"No, we can't. So there's two really important projects that could use your input," Daisy wheedled.

"All right. But I'm still buying the Martin place. I really like the location."

"Dad!" She couldn't bear to think of her father out there alone. "This house is big enough for all of us, even if Ty and Jade decided to move in with us."

"Nope. I've made up my mind. I love real estate, and the Martin place needs my attention."

"I don't like it. The babies need their grandfather." Family was so important. But today was clearly the day for the men in her life to be stubborn mules. "Will you at least go try to talk some sense into my husband?"

He shook his head. "My days of meddling are over. I leave that up to the younger crew. I'm going to be happy as a local real estate fixer-upper. Once that storm came through town, I realized I had a new mission. Putting this town back together," Robert said happily.

"Dad, if John doesn't win, I'm not sure what will happen."

"Yes, but that's what makes life interesting." Robert rose, kissed her on the forehead. "You worry too much, daughter. Let your fellow be your handsome prince on his holy grail if that's what he wants. You have to admire a man with that much getalong in his hindquarters. Wish I'd had it when I was married to your mother," he said, retreating from the room. She heard him and Barclay chatting up a storm in the kitchen—as much as Barclay chatted—which turned into a discussion of a noon libation and a good lunch for her father. Daisy shook her head. It didn't even sound like her father was going down to the race.

"And I'm here, like Sleeping Beauty, consigned to

resting and waiting for my prince. Argh!" She lay back, putting a hand on her tummy. The boys were doing gymnastics inside her, and Daisy smiled.

These little guys were going to be just like their father: busy, strong and opinionated.

And no doubt daredevils who couldn't resist a challenge.

John loved a challenge. And just for once, she was the prize at the end of it.

She lay back, resting, her smile huge.

Yet so many things could go wrong.

She picked up her phone and dialed Cosette.

"WE ALL TRIED to talk him out of it," Cosette said, when Daisy told her that she didn't need a big day, she didn't need anything. She just wanted John, and her babies. Nothing mattered to her but them. Of course her father and the townspeople and Bridesmaids Creek mattered to her, but for once in her life she had exactly what she'd always dreamed of—and her Prince Charming was off to the races.

"You have to do something, Cosette. Please!"

"Not me. I interfered last time, remember? Had him tied to a tree?" She giggled with delight. "Your gang of gentlemen loved that assignment, I can tell you!"

"You can't tie him this time, he'll be ready for tricks." Daisy thought quickly. "What if we waylay all five members of my gang?"

"I think John would suspect that you're trying to let him win, honey," Cosette said gently. "You're just going to have to let this play out."

"Cosette, from a matchmaker's apprentice to a matchmaker, you know better than anyone that the art to matchmaking is making sure that things go a certain way. This time, I really need your help."

"Yes, but you're the matchmaker now," Cosette said with a happy sigh. "I've officially turned over my wand."

"I haven't even made a match yet."

"I have great faith in the five ladies you picked out for your gang. They'll be delighted. And I heard you sent the ladies to the salon and had them beautified and transformed for their big day, courtesy of a certain secret benefactor, who I happen to know is Daisy Donovan." Cosette giggled gleefully. "The girls were thrilled. I peeked in, and they looked smashing. The fellows are going to swim their hearts out."

"You appreciate that I caught myself in my own game?"

"Oh, yes. That's what makes it so delicious! That SEAL husband of yours is going to have real competition this time, once your gang gets a look at the lovely prizes they're swimming for!" Cosette's laugh was merry.

Daisy grimaced. "They won't be able to outswim John."

"You hope. Otherwise—"

"About that otherwise," Daisy said. "What exactly happens if a man is married, swims and doesn't win? Cisco won when he was married to Suz, so do we even have precedent in BC for this?"

"No, we don't, which makes it very exciting!"

"Not if you're the one who wants to keep your husband! You realize I can't get off this sofa. I won't know a thing about what's happening!"

"That's the way it should be, I think. You don't want to be there if John gets another, er, ah—"

"Don't even say it." Daisy wasn't sure what would happen if John lost. Maybe nothing.

Maybe everything.

"In the olden days they said the charm was what built this town," Cosette said. "There was magic in the water, in the very earth of Bridesmaids Creek. Of course, Jane's great-great-great-grandmother settled this town, as you know, and she was the one who knew the secrets. Discovered them, you might say."

"Or maybe Eliza Chatham was just a great story-teller," Daisy reasoned.

"I wouldn't bet on it. Rumor has it that Eliza wanted a match of her own, but it was years before one came along for her." Cosette let out a gentle sigh. "By the time her prince came along, Eliza had two gentlemen vying for her hand."

"What happened?" Daisy asked breathlessly.

"Well, they swam for her, of course."

"And she married the winner."

"Right there on the banks of Bridesmaids Creek. That was the deal. That was how they solved the problem of which man would win her hand."

"But didn't she like one man more than the other?"

"It was a different day and time, Daisy. Back then a woman just needed to be married by a certain age, or she was considered a liability to the family. Or odd. A leftover. And as you know, our town has never been full of men." Cosette giggled again. "Personally, I think the race goes back to the days of yore when men fought over a woman. We just have a more gentle way of going about it. Plus all that survival of the fittest stuff plays into it, too. Natural selection and all that. Obviously a woman wanted the strongest, most intelligent mate to father her children."

"I can't imagine not making up my own mind."

"Well, you didn't really," Cosette said. "If you think about it, you thought you wanted another man. John happened to be the fittest mate for you. And today, he's going to prove it once and for all!"

"I hope you're right." Daisy didn't want to think about what might happen if he didn't win.

"How are you feeling, anyway, my dear?"

"Like I'm full of babies."

"Which you are!" Cosette sounded delighted. "You lie there and rest, and I'll bring you some of my fresh gingerbread cake after the race!"

"Cosette, I expect you to text me every single event that transpires! Don't you dare leave me hanging without any news!"

"This is more fun than we've had in years in BC," Cosette said. "Don't you worry, Daisy. Your reputation as a matchmaker will be secure after today, I just know it! Ta-ta!"

Cosette rang off. Daisy put her phone away and leaned back. It wasn't about the matchmaking, it was about her marriage. Maybe there was no such thing as a charm. Maybe Bridesmaids Creek wasn't charmed at all.

She knew better.

All she'd ever wanted was to belong to Bridesmaids Creek. She'd wanted the magic that the other brides had known—it was impossible to miss their happiness and joy on the day each of them had been "won" by their suitor. More than that, even, she'd wanted to be a true daughter of Bridesmaids Creek, accepted and loved.

The only reason she'd ever acted out, acted differently from the other girls, was that she'd always known she was an outsider.

After today, if John lost, she'd still be an outsider.

Maybe she wasn't meant to belong.

She hoped that wasn't the case. She had a lot of friends she wanted to make, a lot of good things she wanted to do for Bridesmaids Creek. It was her home. She loved it here.

Her heart was here, and now even more so with John and her babies.

Suz walked in the room, followed by her sister, Mackenzie.

"Hi!" Daisy said, surprised. She sat up. "Why aren't you at the big race?"

Suz put a platter of cookies on the table. Mackenzie smiled. "We already have our men," she said. "We thought we'd come and keep you company while you wait for yours to return."

Daisy's heart glowed inside her like a Christmas star. "I'm so glad you're here."

"I've been in the same position you're in now. Bet you're ready to get off that sofa."

"I am." Daisy looked up as Jade Harper and her mother, Betty, walked into the room.

"We come bearing gifts," Jade said, setting down a large hamper topped with a big blue bow.

Daisy felt tears start to swim in her eyes. "Thank you. Thank you all so much."

"We thought we'd have an impromptu baby shower while the men are amusing themselves being competitive," Betty said. "We haven't had a baby shower in a long time!"

"But, then," Suz said as Barclay came in carrying a large box full of white-and-silver wrapped gifts, "we realized we hadn't had a bachelorette shower for you yet, either. So we had the idea that we'd have a double shower!"

Barclay had retreated after putting the basket down, but now he returned with a silver platter with a pitcher of tea and several crystal glasses.

"This is wonderful," Daisy said. "This is… You're the best," she told them, looking around at her friends—and then it hit her.

They really were her friends.

At some point, Suz and Mackenzie, though they'd once deemed her too wild for their circle, had accepted her. Liked her, even. And so had Jade Harper, and her mother, Betty. Jane Chatham and Cosette, too—they were her friends.

She was no longer an outsider.

She truly was a daughter of Bridesmaids Creek. By the genuine smiles on their faces, Daisy knew that she would never, ever be on the outside again. No matter what happened today with the race, everything, absolutely everything, was going to be magical, from this day forward.

And that was the real gift.

THE STARTING LINE seemed full of meatheads, or at least that was John's opinion. He had this—he had it in the bag. Today was his day, he was golden, and he was going to give Daisy the day she deserved, and all the magic that went along with it.

He could beat these guys. He was a SEAL, he was in top condition.

And he was in love. He could run all day.

Just thinking about Daisy and his boys made him want to run to New York and back. Montana, California, he could just keep going.

Only he didn't have to anymore. Home was right here, in Bridesmaids Creek, with Daisy.

He looked over at Dig, Carson, Clint, Red and Gabriel.

"You realize you're going down," Carson said.

"You just keep thinking that," John shot back.

"Might as well just stand right there and save your strength," Red said.

"Keep talking," John told Daisy's gang. "It's all over but the crying."

"Hope you drank your special anti-leg-cramp juice this morning," Dig said.

John laughed. "You fellows. I'm going to throw confetti at all your weddings after today."

"Today we're going to prove that Daisy made a mistake. She shouldn't have married you," Gabriel said. "Any of us would have been a better choice."

"That's okay, boys. I know I got the best girl in town. You just swim your little hearts out and try not to let the waves I send back on you blow you out of the creek." John felt pretty good about his chances. All the smack-talking felt great, too. He enjoyed the brotherhood and camaraderie of small-town rivalry.

And it was all for Daisy. He wouldn't have had it any other way. Spectators lined the banks of the creek, waving posters with the combatants' names on them, cheering occasionally. The Haunted H might be gone from these banks thanks to the storm, but they'd rebuild it here, bigger and better. Everyone loved coming to Bridesmaids Creek, for the community and the happy endings, and yes, the fairy tales. There was a lot of fairy tale in BC, and it charmed him just as much as anyone else.

To his astonishment, he spotted his mother, father and brothers on the banks, too, waving a banner with his name on it. John grinned. Oh, this had Daisy's fingerprints all over it. She was all about family, and it warmed his heart in the best way that she wanted to be a part of his family, too.

"On your mark!" Sheriff McAdams called. John took a deep breath. "Get set!"

The pistol fired, and John took off like a Navy SEAL on a mission. He could hear the guys next to him churning up the water, flailing away, but he never had a doubt that there would only be one winner today.

This race, this day, was for Daisy, the most beautiful bride a man could ever have.

He felt great, swimming along like a salmon in a hurry. A roar went up from the banks, but he didn't stop, he kept on going.

At the finish line, he touched, came to the surface with a huge gasp for air. Sam pulled him out of the water.

"Congrats, old son! You did it!" Sam told him, trying to hand him a towel.

"Damn right I did," John said, and took off running down the road.

Behind him he could hear the roars growing louder. He heard car engines and a general melee breaking out. But he kept going, until he reached Best Man's Fork. Up ahead he could see Sheriff McAdams in his truck, keeping an eye on the proceedings. Cosette and Jane were in the truck with him, and he thought he saw Jane videotaping him as he jogged down Best Man's Fork.

He ran the entire length of the race, if it had been a running race today, making sure everyone knew when they told this story over the years that this was the SEAL, this was the groom, who not only swam to win his bride, but ran to win her, too.

Daisy's gang had given up long ago, presumably taking the time to eye the lovely women Daisy'd had at the finish line that they hadn't won today. They would have had to beat him to win their special ladies, but they hadn't, so their stories would have to wait.

Today was all about Daisy.

He crossed the finish line, puffing for breath. The sheriff pulled up alongside him, with Sam in the back. Sam handed him a water bottle, which John grabbed gratefully.

"Remind you of the old days?" Sam asked. "Training until you dropped?"

"Not yet," John said, and took off jogging for home.

He had no intention of stopping until he ran right into Daisy Donovan Mathison's welcoming arms.

And that was his happy ending.

Chapter Seventeen

Daisy let out a yelp when her husband roared into the den where she was having a lovely tea and bridal/baby shower with the ladies. John looked wild, his hair askew, sweaty as all get-out—and he'd never looked better to her.

"Excuse me, ladies, I have to kiss my bride," John said, and Daisy flung her arms around his neck as he came to get a winner's smooch.

"That was something else," Jane said, following John in with Cosette and Sheriff McAdams on her heels. "I wish you'd seen this bowlegged cowboy run, Daisy. He sure can get a move on."

"Really?" Daisy grinned at her husband. "I thought it was a swim I organized for today."

"I swam, I ran, I lived up to any charm Bridesmaids Creek cares to throw at me," he bragged. "I'm all about the magic, beautiful."

"And now you're stuck with him," Sheriff Dennis said, and Suz handed everyone a glass of tea so they could toast the newlyweds.

"It was really special," Cosette said. "We have it all on video, so you can show your sons exactly what their father did for love."

Daisy beamed, feeling so much joy pour into her. She didn't think she'd ever been happier. "Thank you, John."

"It was nothing," he said, and everyone in the room laughed, because it was more than something.

It was everything.

"Wow, look at all these booties and teddy bears." John was amazed by all the wonderful gifts stacked around. He held up a teddy of a different sort, filmy and white and lacy. Daisy blushed a bit. "This isn't for my sons," John said.

Everyone laughed again, but Daisy saw a spark of something she remembered very well jump into her husband's eyes.

"It won't be too long before I fit into that," Daisy said. "Just a few months."

John laid the sexy teddy back down. "Clearly someone in this room wants me to have a heart attack. And I'm going to enjoy every second of it."

They dug into the cookies and tea, and sat around sharing stories and enjoying each other's company. John went to shower, and when he returned, his parents had arrived for the party.

Daisy held her breath, but John went right to his family, wrapping them in big hugs. Robert milled around, introducing himself.

Her big, sexy husband loved her enough to make sure she had her own magical day.

He plopped down next to her, leaning over to give her a smooch that curled her toes and left her breathless.

"So, Mrs. Mathison, you're certainly full of surprises."

"Yes. And I plan to keep on surprising you." She looked at him. "You had a few surprises yourself. What inspired you to run the Fork, too?"

"You, beautiful." He kissed her full on the lips. "And the sheer joy of beating your gang all over again. Setting up a record so big they'll never be able to touch it." He grinned. "And I outdid even my SEAL brothers."

"Yes, you did." She laughed. "You're part of BC history, now."

He sat up. "I am. I'm part of BC history now!"

She smiled. "I'm glad that makes you happy."

"You have *no* idea."

He had a funny little smile on his face, and Daisy wasn't sure what it meant—but the smile left in a hurry when she kissed him long and slow and sweet. Their guests applauded, and Daisy knew that, even if she'd never thought she'd have her big day, the magic had woven its spell for her just the way she'd always dreamed.

And it was absolutely, completely Bridesmaids Creek–perfect.

OF COURSE THE babies were in just as much of a hurry as their father had been, and John found himself the recipient of three bundles of joy a week later. He could hardly believe it, but he had three—three!—sons of his own to hold.

It was a miracle. In fact, it was magical.

"Daisy, look at their toes!" John couldn't believe anything could have toes so tiny. And their fingers were so small he couldn't believe they would ever hold a baseball, rope a steer, play a guitar or touch a woman.

But they'd grow.

He looked at his beautiful wife. "You're the most amazing woman on the planet. I swear I'm the luckiest guy around."

"You are." Daisy glowed at the praise. "I'm pretty lucky myself."

He couldn't stop staring at the babies. The nurses had to convince him to let them take them to the neonatal nursery, and finally they shooed him out of the OR so they could finish whatever it was they were doing to Daisy. Delivery by C-section was supposed to have been the best choice, considering they'd suddenly decided the babies needed to be born. There'd been a question of heartbeats and distress, and John had known a few moments of terror, but it had all worked out. Now he had three healthy boys. They'd stay in the hospital for a few weeks while their lungs became more developed, but even so, John thought his sons were perfect.

So was his wife. He followed the nurse down the hall to wait in the room where Daisy would be, pacing until they finally wheeled her in.

"I love you," he told her. "The best thing that ever happened in my life is you. Hands down."

A luminous smile brightened her face, though he could tell she was tired. "I hope you've picked out names."

"Names!" John straightened. "You're the matchmaker, you do the picking. But please do it quickly. I didn't realize we had no names for our boys!"

The nurse, overhearing all this, laughed. "You can take a few days if you need to."

"That's all right," Daisy said. "I was thinking John, Cisco and Sam for first names. We could choose Robert, Justin and Tyson for second names. We want to include your father, as well," she continued, but John waved a hand.

"Why is Sam part of this?"

"Don't you know?" she asked curiously.

"Know what?"

"Sam helped Cosette set everything up for all you guys. Laid the traps, he called it. You, Cisco and Ty—"

"Were like lambs being led to their shepherd," Sam said, walking in, his arms full of teddy bears.

"Hey, buddy," John said, slapping his friend on the back. "You already brought us one bear. In Austin, remember?"

"What's an uncle without a bear?" Sam grinned. "Besides, these are monogrammed with each baby's name on them."

Squint lifted a brow. "We just chose names. How can they be monogrammed?"

"Cosette told me their names." Sam held up a cute brown bear with a blue T-shirt. "This one's named Sam. But I call him Handsome."

"Oh, brother." John shook his head. "Don't tell me. The other two are named Cisco and John."

"How'd you know?" Sam went to kiss Daisy's cheek. "I just stopped by to see the little cowboys. They've already roped the nurses like true wranglers."

Daisy took a bear from Sam. "I wish you weren't leaving, Sam."

"Leaving?" John perked up, his heart dropping a bit. "Leaving for what?"

"Hitting the road, buddy. My job here is done."

"You can't go. We haven't paid you back for what you did to us," John said. "I mean, for us."

"I'm going." Sam's grin went huge. "I'm not the marrying kind, like I've always said."

"I really wish you wouldn't, Sam," Daisy said. "But I understand, too. Everyone has to find their dream."

"I guess." John frowned. "But we're a team. The three of us stick together."

"I'll be around." Sam kissed Daisy on the cheek, thumped him on the back and went down the hall, whistling.

He looked at Daisy. "You knew he was leaving?"

She nodded. "He'll be back one day. Bridesmaids Creek doesn't leave anyone untouched."

"I hope so." John was a little dumbfounded that his friend had hung around just long enough to see his babies born. "It's not fair that he gets away without getting dragged to the altar."

Daisy laughed. "Yeah, like you were dragged."

"We're getting married again this summer. I hope you know that. With full regalia. Wedding dress, lots of guests, huge cake. The works. Just like we said we would." John considered that for a moment. "You know, I never asked Sam if he really is certified to perform weddings. You can't trust him, you know."

"Oh, you can trust him. You always have."

It was true. No one had your back like Sam. Now that he looked back over their time in Bridesmaids Creek, he realized Sam had been doing the same thing he had when they'd been serving: keeping everybody in line, moving forward, spirits light, eyes on the prize.

"He needs a wife," John grumbled. "It's the least we could do for him. Ask Ty and Cisco if they don't agree."

She took a long drink of water, lay back against the pillow. "So, did you know that my dad bought the Martin place?"

"The ghost house?" He shuddered. "I'd be a little superstitious about that."

"You're superstitious about everything." Daisy's eyes drooped. "Dad's got big plans for that place."

"Your father always has a big plan working."

"And he's put Betty Harper in business selling her frosted Christmas cookies through mail order. She and Jade are going to be growing as fast as she can bake and design."

"You know, I live in this town. I live with you. I should know something that's going on," John said.

"You've been busy. I think you slept for a week after the big races."

"I could do it again tomorrow," he bragged. "But I feel like Rip van Winkle. I woke up, and everything had changed."

"It's Dad. He says that now that he has all these grand-children, he's got a lot to do."

He shook his head. "We'd better put him to work babysitting as soon as we can, before he decides to buy another town or something."

Daisy's eyes were starting to flutter closed. "I'm going to sleep now, my sexy husband."

He touched her skin, needing to connect with her. "When you wake up, beautiful, I'll still be your sexy husband. Just like the prince in the fairy tale. See how that works?"

Daisy rolled her eyes, her lips curved in a gentle smile, and the next thing he knew, a deep, sweet snoring came from his beautiful bride.

This was bliss. This was heaven. John sank down into the chair next to her and held her hand for a moment. He was a father. She'd made him a dad. And he had three sons.

How great was that? For as long as he could remember, he'd wanted a home, a place that was solid, one hearth to call his own. And he had that and more now.

John pulled off his boots to ease the blisters he'd developed the day he'd run all over Bridesmaids Creek to win his bride, and realized Sam had left one last gift behind, pinned to one of the teddy bear's ears.

He reached for the small envelope and opened the note.

John, ol' son, when I first met you, I thought you were the most hammerheaded dunce I'd ever met. Then you saved my life with that squint eye of yours. I can still hear the shots you squeezed off, and how you hit those marks I'll never know. No one shoots like you do, that's for sure. I guess you're still shooting good, or you wouldn't have those three bundles of joy. That's the thing about you, John, you're steadfast, you hang in there until the end, after everyone else has quit and gone home. You're a friend, a good man and you'll be a helluva father. Be happy, stay sane and always remember home is where the heart is. It was the only thing you were missing. And now you've got it. Congratulations. Three little boys to follow your footsteps and learn from you, and become men like their dad. I call that a happy-as-hell ending. Sam

John closed his eyes. Shoved the note into his pocket. And picked up Daisy's hand again, placing it over his heart.

Sam was right: it was a happy-as-hell ending.

"So I never did figure out exactly what an unmatch-maker does," John said, a month later, after they'd brought the boys home from the hospital and began settling them into the castle where his princess lived. John was getting used to living in the Donovan mansion, though some days he felt as if he needed a compass and a treasure map just to find the kitchen.

"An unmatchmaker unmakes matches." Daisy looked at him as she finished diapering little John.

He sat down, popping the bottle into John's mouth right before he let out the squall of the century. "But there aren't any matches in BC that were unmade, except for Mackenzie's—"

"Which wasn't Cosette's fault."

"And Cosette's own match."

Daisy nodded. "I know. It's hard to feel like we've had a happy ending without Cosette and Phillipe being together. So much of that feels like it was my fault."

John didn't think so. "I ran for them, too, you know. I thought that if we could get the magic back in Cosette's wand, get her belief in herself back, she and Phillipe might find their way back together. Which would be good for Bridesmaids Creek."

Daisy went to lay her head against his shoulder. "You did your best. And everyone knows it. You're a huge part of BC because of it." She leaned up to kiss him. "And I love you for it."

Life didn't get better than a wife kissing you until you could feel your insides practically melting from love, desire, anticipation—everything that was Daisy.

He sneaked his hands into the waistband of her skirt, the promise of "later" revving his heart rate further.

"Daze, I'm going out to Phillipe's for a while. He

wants me to help him look over an area of his yard for some chicken coops. He's decided he wants to raise his own organic chicken. Really going granola, is Phillipe."

"We'll all be eating farm-fresh eggs soon. Go ahead and go. Your family's coming over to dote on the babies for a bit."

"They've stayed in BC a little longer than I thought they would." John looked at Daisy. "Did you notice?"

"I did." She had a big smile on her face. "I think they want to talk to you about staying on here."

John raised a brow. "Staying on?"

She nodded, her eyes twinkling. "Putting down stakes in BC, is how they put it."

"My parents, who have never owned a house that didn't move, want to put down stakes." He was stunned. "I didn't see that coming."

"They really like it here. Your brothers, too. They want to help with the rebuilding of the Haunted H down on the creek, and I think Justin's been hiring them to do some stuff at the Hanging H, especially helping with the roof repairs."

"My brothers can do anything." When you lived on the road, you learned a lot of do-it-yourself handyman skills. "That's awesome. I'm glad to hear it."

"Are you?"

"Yeah. Thrilled, actually. It's great news."

Daisy wore a pleased expression. "There's another draw to BC for your family, apparently."

"Oh?" He could tell his bride was holding back the big news.

"Yes. They're a bit fascinated with the matchmaking lore in our small town."

He grinned. "Looking to settle down, are they?"

"It seems that the idea of families of their own appeals to Javier and Jackson. And your parents love the idea of settling where there's a lot of grandchildren."

"I can't believe it. Who would have ever thought all it would take to get my family off the road was a bunch of babies?"

Daisy laughed. "Our babies settled us down."

He loved her, that was all there was to it. She was so happy to call herself settled, to be a mother and a wife. "I love you."

"I know." She smiled. "And lucky for you, your entire family is staying here tonight to babysit."

He raised a brow. "Why is that lucky for me?"

She got up, came to slide her arms around his neck. "Because tonight we're going to have our honeymoon night, husband. I've got that lacy teddy you liked so much packed and ready to go."

His heart started beating real hard. "You're sure?"

"I'm sure, the doctor's sure. Everyone's sure."

He sucked in a breath, felt his whole body responding to her. "Daisy, you drive me wild, beautiful."

He kissed her, drinking in the moment. Daisy and he, well, it had been worth the wait. She'd tried real hard to outrun him, but somehow he'd always known that this woman was the only woman for him.

His heart always beat faster when she was around. Like right now, beating like crazy. Felt like a motorcycle in a fast lane, going hard to its destination. And the funny thing was how good it felt, as if everything in his life was exactly perfect now.

John Lopez "Squint" Mathison had made it home, for good.

SEVERAL HOURS LATER, John made it back to the underground cave. There was one thing he had to know, and this was where he'd find the answer.

The cave was completely deserted, although he wouldn't have been surprised to find Jane here. She appeared to be the keeper of the ledger, and Cosette was the keeper of the legend. Eventually, he'd figure out what his role in all this was to be, but for now, he wanted to know if the magic finally accepted him.

He approached the table, pulled the ledger out of its hiding place. It fell open easily, surprising him.

He sat down, turned a page, and started reading where he'd left off when the book had sealed itself before.

> Somehow I knew when I first arrived here that this place was my new home. We were hot and dusty from travel on the wagon, but most of the people decided to push on. I felt my heart beating harder here, racing with excitement, the moment I stepped down from the wagon and my feet touched the soil.
>
> I decided to stay, and so did Thomas.

John looked up. There'd been no mention of a Thomas previously. He checked the tree in the front of the book quickly—no Thomas. He went back to Eliza's fine, spare handwriting.

> We might not have made it past a few days if Hiram hadn't come to see what the newcomers to the area were doing. How he must have laughed at our efforts. Thomas being from New York was

hardly versed in how to survive on a prairie, and though I had nursing skills and knowledge of vegetation and cooking, settling was daunting.

At first we were a bit unsure about this tall, dark-skinned man with the darkly electric eyes, but it was clear Hiram was educated and meant us no harm. Hiram said later that he'd only come to help us because I wore a pretty blue dress, unlike any blue he'd ever seen outside of the creek, which he later led us to so we could get fresh water.

I think secretly Thomas hoped I'd give up on my adventure and return home, once the Texas heat and estrangement from my family wore me down. I can only say that, for my part, every day I grew more excited about my new home. And Hiram's assistance made our settling go that much easier.

Soon we had a shelter built, a very small house, with a room partitioned for me and one for Thomas. He very much hoped I'd accept his suit, but without any family here, it didn't seem as important to me as it once had. Marriage was a lifetime commitment, and for the moment, I was committed to this new world that fascinated me.

To my surprise, once people passing through on their way to farther off destinations saw our small house and the land we were clearing, a few more decided to stay. Within six months, we had neighbors of a sort.

Thomas, however, had grown impatient. I realized he very much hoped to be back home for Christmas. I had no intention of leaving Texas.

We were at an impasse—and then Hiram offered a suggestion, surprising me.

He challenged Thomas to a race, to win my hand.

Thomas did not accept that challenge outright, as he believed I would not be interested in the suit of a man from a tribe, an Indian whose way of life was so different from what the two of us had known.

But in my heart, I felt a strong, strange connection to Hiram—even though I wasn't sure his name was actually Hiram, or if that was just a name he gave us to sound civilized. He'd been tutored by some priests who had passed through their grounds over the years, and so he was quite comfortable with our language and our customs. If not for the fact that he was obviously a native, one would not have known by his manners and refinement.

He was tall and strong, and well built, his face honest with its dark eyes and the clear intelligence he'd shown. I knew he liked to laugh—while Thomas was of a more serious bent.

I accepted Hiram's offer. Reluctantly, Thomas did, as well.

They agreed to swim the creek for my hand. Some of our new neighbors came to watch. It was a close race, as Thomas was fit, but Hiram knew the waters better, and I believe swam with more purpose. To be honest, I think Thomas had begun to realize over time that I was not the bride he sought; I would never be happy in a refined drawing-room setting. Already I was eager to visit the village where the natives were and use my nursing skills to help, and learn from their style of preparing food. Thomas had no interest in the community, and I believe he didn't compete with the same fervor as he once might have.

I don't know that for a fact, of course. It's only a suspicion.

Secretly, I was terribly glad Hiram won that day. I have been, ever since. He's a good man, and he treats me well. His tribe let me know I was welcome. We settled not far from the creek, and it's so beautiful here that some nights I just sit and stare at the stars and wonder what my life would have been like if I hadn't come here.

As far as I am concerned, it's magic.

John stopped reading, surprised by the story and yet somehow not surprised. All the women in Bridesmaids Creek were strong and independent; the founder had certainly set the precedent for courage and steady determination. He leafed back to the tree, seeing that Eliza had several children, three girls, one boy.

Even back then, BC was destined to be a woman's town.

He read that she'd named Bridesmaids Creek and then Best Man's Fork, after she and Hiram were married. It seemed romantic, and besides, the creek was how she'd come to have a husband. John learned that back home Eliza had been in several weddings, and folks had teased her that she might be destined to "always be a bridesmaid and never a bride." But they'd been wrong.

The footpath of the Fork became a very special spot

for her and her beloved husband. They walked it often, gazing up at the stars and listening to the crickets and cicadas.

"Hi," he heard suddenly, and John looked up to see Daisy standing in the cave entrance. She looked like an angel, and his heart skipped a beat.

"Hello, wife." Closing the ledger, he stood, walked straight to Daisy. "Fancy meeting you in this place."

"Cosette said I might find you here," Daisy said, her face a little awed as she glanced around. "This is amazing. How did you ever find it?"

John grinned. "The same way you did. Cosette and Jane."

"So this is where you were going the night the tornado hit. You were coming here to check on it."

John wrapped her in his arms. "Once the ladies and the sheriff admitted me to their secret club, I felt a duty to make sure it stayed safe."

Daisy looked up at him. "It's what you do best. Keep things safe."

He loved the sound of that. He loved her holding him in her arms. "You realize we're the new Madame Matchmaker and Monsieur Unmatchmaker? I don't think there's any way of getting away from it, now that we've been shown the secrets of Bridesmaids Creek."

Daisy tucked her head against his shoulder, close to his heart. "I think that's exactly what we were always meant to be. It just took us a while to figure it out." She looked up at him. "By the way, Cosette and Phillipe got back together. They're getting married next weekend, and they've invited Sam back to do the honors."

"That seems appropriate. Sam's going to figure out eventually that Bridesmaids Creek has no intention of letting him go. That's just not what our town does. Once you're here, you belong."

"And I'm so glad."

They walked to the cave entrance together, holding each other. This was heaven. He could have kept living everywhere and anywhere, but with Daisy and his children, he'd found home.

They looked up as a shower of stars fell from the sky. Daisy laughed with delight, and John held his matchmaking bride close. It was magical here, and Daisy was magical, and John Lopez "Squint" Mathison might have been superstitious as hell, as his friends always said, but he'd always believed in magic.

And in Bridesmaids Creek, love was the magic.

Which made for a happy ending, every time.

Epilogue

Sam found himself performing another wedding ceremony, this time for John and Daisy on a beautiful July day, when cicadas sang in the trees and crickets chirped at dusk by the creek. It was the perfect music to accompany Daisy on Robert's arm, as he walked her toward John, who stood waiting for his wife under a canopy of oak trees that had probably been around for the past two hundred years. Maybe as long ago as when Bridesmaids Creek had been settled and named by Eliza Chatham.

Daisy was always beautiful, a stunner, but today she was a vision in a long white gown, her chocolate locks caressed by a veil flowing down her back. She carried a beautiful bouquet of white roses and greenery, and as she came to stand at his side, John caught his breath, falling in love with his wife all over again.

Every day he loved her more. And his babies had sucked him into their busy worlds, drawing his heart further in with every breath they took.

Their families and friends grouped around to watch the wedding, and John felt the blessing of their presence. Since the big storm, the town had become closer. Working together, they'd rebuilt the Hanging H, and the Haunted H had come back bigger and better than ever along the creek, drawing more visitors than ever. The sheriff's jail had been completed, so "fancy," as Dennis said, that it was more of a hotel than a jail—not that anyone ever spent any time there except to visit him.

Cosette and Phillipe had their original shops back. Phillipe was teaching yoga in his shop, and Cosette taught deportment classes, which she called cotillion, on her side, and reopened the tearoom. Though she'd definitely gotten her matchmaking groove back, she left the matchmaking business up to Daisy, and that gave John plenty of time to watch his wife finagle unsuspecting victims up to the wedding altar. She'd already had two very successful matches so far: the first, her father, Robert, to Betty Harper. John had never seen that one coming, but Daisy wisely had, right about the time she mentioned to her father that Betty's frosted Christmas cookies would be awesome in a mail-order business. His entrepreneurial-minded wife had been right—and the cookies proved an easy way to get Robert and Betty to see each other in a new light, which was something, considering the row they'd once had long ago.

The meatheads—Daisy's gang, John reminded himself—had talked Robert into selling them the Martin place. A ghost-riddled house was the perfect place to set up their cigar bar establishment, they claimed, so Robert sold it to them and stayed on at the Donovan compound. That was fine with John. He was comfortable with lots of people around. His parents had bought Phillipe's house once he moved in with Cosette, and Javier and Jackson were staying at the Hanging H bunkhouse, with Justin finding that they were more than handy and welcome on the team. It was great having his family around, and they spent every second with the babies that they could, which brought them all closer together as a family, something John treasured.

He didn't shed a single tear when the old silver family trailer found its way to a buyer, and rolled off for the last time. For his family, he bought a van, and told Daisy it would never be used for distances greater than visiting family and friends.

Mackenzie and Justin had once thought they'd never need additional hands at the Hanging H, but now business was booming, thanks to the Haunted H going so well. People came from miles around to look at the beautiful Hanging H, which had become something of a monument to the town. The Hawthornes would have been proud and awed by how their daughters had kept the family business going, and supporting Bridesmaids Creek.

Daisy's second match had been to fix Jackson up with one of the local girls, a sweet librarian who was compiling all the family's road adventures into a book and a video. Though he'd never thought their family life was all that interesting, it turned out that people were fascinated by how a family could be raised on the road. There were already offers on the project to publish the book and do something with the video, much to John's astonishment.

But he was more interested in life in Bridesmaids Creek.

John loved taking his babies on jogs, staying in shape the way a SEAL needed to do. He'd developed a stroller that would accommodate three babies safely, and every Saturday, he took them for a run down Best Man's Fork. It was the most peaceful, serene time of his week, and the babies loved it. To his surprise, his jog had caught on with the town. First his SEAL brothers started out joining him with their broods, and that had made for a nice-sized group. Then the wives decided to join in, and that led to their friends coming out, too. Soon they had so many people coming out on the weekends to run the Best Man's Fork that they decided to turn it into an annual charity marathon, because if there was one thing Bridesmaids Creek did really well, it was take care of each other, and anyone who might have a need of a helping hand. The charity was hugely successful, keeping John busy.

But not too busy to be a great husband and father. He smiled at his darling wife as Sam began the wedding ceremony. Daisy smiled back up at him, her eyes full of love, and John knew he was the luckiest man in the whole world.

"I love you," he whispered.

"Excuse me," Sam said, grinning. "I'm trying to conduct a wedding."

Daisy smiled. "I love you, too, my big hunky husband." She stood on her toes to kiss him, and John breathed her in, held her tight, his heart expanding with joy. He heard Sam laugh and the guests applaud, but he didn't let go of Daisy. *This* was the magic he'd always wanted.

And he was never, ever letting her go.

Because this was Bridesmaids Creek. The magic had always been here, right where he and Daisy had hoped to find it.

They were finally home.

Together, forever.

* * * * *

MILLS & BOON®

The Rising Stars Collection!

1 BOOK FREE!

This fabulous four-book collection features 3-in-1 stories from some of our talented writers who are the stars of the future! Feel the temperature rise this summer with our ultra-sexy and powerful heroes. Don't miss this great offer—buy the collection today to get one book free!

**Order yours at
www.millsandboon.co.uk/risingstars**

Don't miss Sarah Morgan's
next Puffin Island story

Some Kind of Wonderful

Brittany Forrest has stayed away from Puffin Island
since her relationship with Zach Flynn went bad.
They were married for ten days and only just
managed not to kill each other by the
end of the honeymoon.

But, when a broken arm means she must return,
Brittany moves back to her Puffin Island home.
Only to discover that Zac is there as well.

Will a summer together help two lovers reunite or
will their stormy relationship crash on to the
rocks of Puffin Island?

Some Kind of Wonderful
COMING JULY 2015
Pre-order your copy today

Join our *EXCLUSIVE* eBook club

FROM JUST £1.99 A MONTH!

Never miss a book again with our hassle-free eBook subscription.

★ Pick how many titles you want from each series with our flexible subscription

★ Your titles are delivered to your device on the first of every month

★ Zero risk, zero obligation!

There really is nothing standing in the way of you and your favourite books!

Start your eBook subscription today at www.millsandboon.co.uk/subscribe

MILLS & BOON®

Cherish™

EXPERIENCE THE ULTIMATE RUSH OF FALLING IN LOVE

A sneak peek at next month's titles...

In stores from 17th July 2015:

- **The Texas Ranger's Bride** – Rebecca Winters *and* **His Unforgettable Fiancée** – Teresa Carpenter

- **The Boss, the Bride & the Baby** – Judy Duarte *and* **Return of the Italian Tycoon** – Jennifer Faye

In stores from 7th August 2015:

- **Do You Take This Maverick?** – Marie Ferrarella *and* **Hired by the Brooding Billionaire** – Kandy Shepherd

- **A Will, a Wish...a Proposal** – Jessica Gilmore *and* **A Reunion and a Ring** – Gina Wilkins

---

Available at WHSmith, Tesco, Asda, Eason, Amazon and Apple

Just can't wait?
Buy our books online a month before they hit the shops!
visit www.millsandboon.co.uk

These books are also available in eBook format!